CONTENTS

Salim Husain Quawwal 5

Painting the Breeze 17

Dal Delight 26

Tenali Rama the Second 36

A Shimmer of Silk 42

Hasan and the Lost Pigeons 57

No Pulao for Nawabsaab 71

Who's Afraid of Ghosts? 80

To Catch a Thief 101

A Sword for Deva Raya 117

HISTORY MYSTERY DAL BIRYANI

SUBHADRA SEN GUPTA

Illustrations
Tapas Guha

SCHOLASTIC
New York Toronto London Auckland
Sydney New Delhi Hong Kong

Subhadra Sen Gupta has written over forty books for children because she thinks children are the best readers in the world. In 2014 she won the Bal Sahitya Puraskar for her children's books. She loves telling stories woven around history, plotting mysteries and adventures, dreaming up ghostly tales and scripting comic books. So if you want to start a conversation with her, write to her at subhadrasg@gmail.com.

Published by Scholastic India Pvt. Ltd.
A subsidiary of Scholastic Inc., New York, 10012 (USA).
Publishers since 1920, with international operations in Canada, Australia, New Zealand, the United Kingdom, India, and Hong Kong.

For information regarding permission, write to:
Scholastic India Pvt. Ltd.
A-27, Ground Floor, Bharti Sigma Centre
Infocity-1, Sector 34, Gurgaon-122001 (India)

First edition: June 2004
This reprint edition: June 2024

ISBN-13: 978-93-5275-533-2

Printed at Ram Printograph Delhi

Salim Husain Quawwal

Salim chose his best dark blue marble and took careful aim at his friend Anwar's best red and white one, when his father yelled from inside, 'Salim!'

'Now what?' Salim sighed, going into the baithak where his father Maqsud Husain sat repairing a tabla. Above the tapping of the small hammer, Maqsud said, 'Run to Balle miyan's house and tell him we will rehearse from tomorrow. He should tell the tabalchi, shehnai player and the chorus.'

Maqsud Husain Dilliwalle was one of the best quawwals in the city of Dilli and Balle miyan was his equally famous sarangi player. They gave concerts not only in town but even went as far as Lucknow and Aligarh. Salim had heard that the crowd had not only been swaying but also dancing to his quawwalis at the last Urs at the tomb of Sheikh Moinuddin Chishti at Ajmer Sharif.

'Another concert?' asked Anwar as the two boys walked to Balle miyan's house in Katra Neel, dodging horses, carts, palkis and people crowding Chandni Chowk. 'Must be,' Salim said wistfully. 'I keep begging abbu to let me join the chorus, but he always says no.'

'Why? You sing pretty well.'

'He says, as the best quawwal in the city of the Mughal badshah Bahadur Shah Zafar, he only takes the best musicians. He thinks I'm too young, and my talim is not complete.' Next morning the boys and Salim's sister Farida were again playing in the courtyard when they saw Maqsud quawwal's music party arrive. Balle miyan came holding his precious sarangi like a baby. Behind him, Akhtar Khan, the tabla player, strolled in chewing paan with Ram Pyare, the shehnai player, and then came the two men who sang in the chorus and kept beat by clapping. After chatting for a few minutes and tuning their instruments, they all settled down to rehearse.

Salim knew all the songs and hummed along as he played. After a while he was singing to the clack of marbles. *'Chhaap tilak sab chhini re ...'* He then pricked up his ears. 'Arrey! They are rehearsing all the Amir Khusro numbers!'

'So?' Anwar asked.

'Don't you understand? That means abbu must be singing at the Urs of Khusro at Nizamuddin this year!'

'At the Urs!' Even Anwar began to get excited. 'You'll be going too, I'm sure. Nizamuddin is not as far as Ajmer. Can I come too?'

'I'll have to ask him.'

That night at dinner, as their mother served them hot rotis and bowls of saag meat, Salim asked his father, 'Abbu, why were you rehearsing Khusro's numbers? Will you be singing at the Urs?'

Maqsud smiled. 'Very smart guess! But you're not singing with me.'

'Please abbu,' Salim pleaded, but Maqsud shook his head again.

'Then at least can we stay late and listen to you?' Farida asked. 'Anwar wants to come too.'

'You always send us back early from Nizamuddin,' Salim's mother complained. 'We never hear you sing.'

'Nahi,' said Maqsud shortly. 'If you stay back, I'll have to hire a room at the sarai for the night.'

'But it's the Urs!' Farida and Salim protested.

'It costs money,' Maqsud ended the argument firmly. For a while they all ate in silence. Then Farida said, 'If I had the money, I'd pay for the sarai.'

Maqsud laughed, 'You couldn't earn it in months.'

'Suppose we do get the money,' their mother said, 'then would you let us stay and listen to you?'

'Of course,' Maqsud's amusement grew. 'Better still, even if you earn half the cost, I'll pay the rest.'

'Done!' said Farida, Salim and their mother in unison.

'You'll never make it,' Maqsud said confidently. 'The Urs is next week!'

Next day, while the house echoed with the quawwalis at the rehearsal, Salim, Farida, their mother and Anwar held a conference in the kitchen.

'I could work at a shop,' Anwar suggested.

'You won't earn anything in a week.'

'We could sell something ...' Salim was thoughtful. 'Kites, toys?'

'Food,' his mother said firmly. 'If I made a big handi of biryani, could you go and sell it at the market near Jama Masjid?'

'Ji ammi!'

'At least twenty helpings at a paisa each,' Farida, the practical one, calculated quickly. 'We could collect the money in a week'.

'But not a word to abbu!' Salim warned.

Early next morning, shivering a bit in the chilly spring air, they got busy. Salim lit the chullah, fanning and coughing in the smoke. Anwar pounded the masala, Farida cleaned the rice. And they sat and watched anxiously as their mother began frying the spices and tender pieces of meat, boiling the rice, straining the saffron. The heavenly smells made them all very hungry!

After tasting the biryani, the children carried the big covered handi of the fragrant dish to Jama Masjid at noon.

'Biryani le lo,' Anwar began yelling.

Farida looked around. The steps leading to the mosque are a busy place with the worshippers going in to pray, the vendors selling trinkets and toys, fruit and clothes, a man putting kohl into people's eyes from a silver bottle and another cleaning their ears. There were food sellers yelling out their wares—roti and kebabs, bright coloured sherbets, laddoos, pedas and zarda, the sweet yellow rice. Two other men selling biryani were giving them suspicious looks.

'Biryani! Come and taste our biryani! Only one paisa!' yodelled Salim.

'Biryani ki bahaar!' shouted one of the men Salim was up against.

'Biryani mazedaar!' called the other.

As the sun climbed the sky, the lunchtime crowd grew. The other two biryani sellers obviously had their regular clientele. Only a few people wandered over to buy from the children. As dusk fell over Chandni Chowk, they had sold only half the handi. Counting the coins, Anwar sighed, 'Only 12 paise!'

'We'll sell more tomorrow,' Salim said. 'Everyone liked ammi's biryani, so they'll come back.'

'And bring their friends,' Anwar added optimistically.

That night there was leftover biryani for dinner. Looking at his heaped plate, Maqsud said, 'Wah! What's the occasion?'

Salim's mother frowned. 'Nothing special!'

'Are you trying to make me change my mind by feeding me biryani?'

'Never!' said Farida. 'Next week we'll pay our expenses. You just wait and see.'

'I will,' Maqsud laughed, not noticing how quiet his son was.

That night Salim pulled the quilt up to his chin, sat up in bed and thought furiously. He stared out of the window onto the moonlight-silver street of Ballimaran as the night became quiet with just the street dogs barking. Then he crept out of bed, lit a candle, found a piece of paper, ink and a pen and laboriously wrote a few lines.

Next morning as they all worked to make more biryani, while fanning the chullah, Salim handed the chit of paper to Anwar and said, 'Learn this by heart.'

Slowly Anwar read out the four lines of wavy handwriting.

Meri yeh biryani laajawab
Kha kar toh dekhiye janaab
Ek paise mein swad ki pudiya
Meri yeh biryani hai badhiya.

'Wah! Wah! A poem for our biryani!' Anwar's eyes shone. 'Do you have a tune for it?'

And Salim, sitting beside the chullah, wreathed in smoke, sang his ode to biryani.

They settled on the masjid steps again. The moment the other biryani sellers saw them, their shouts got louder. Salim pulled out a small dholak that he had sneaked out of his father's music room from under his shawl and they began to sing. He and Farida would sing a line while Anwar clapped to their tune and then joined in with a 'Wah! Wah!' at the end of it.

People turned at the sound of their young voices and Salim's pretty tune and laughed at his awful verse. But they walked over and bought a leaf-plate of biryani.

In a while Salim's song had collected quite a crowd around him and the biryani was selling so fast that Farida had to run home to get another handi of the spicy rice. Just at that time Maqsud Husain left his house after the morning riyaz. He was walking towards the mosque in time for the afternoon prayers. He looked curiously at the huddle of people around a vendor and then heard very familiar voices raised in song.

Meri yeh biryani laajawab!

'What's that?' he wondered. His steps slowed.

Kha kar to dekhiye janaab.

Salim's voice!

Ek paise mein swad ...

And Farida's! And Anwar's!

He pushed himself through the crowd to see a sight that froze him in anger. Salim, the only son of Maqsud Husain, Dilli's famous quawwal, sat there with a handi of biryani, singing a terrible song and beating the dholak like a street singer!

In a second he reached forward, yanked Salim out of the crowd and then whispered angrily, 'What do you think you are doing?'

'Selling biryani. 'We are earning the money for the sarai. You never said we couldn't do it by selling biryani!'

'Come home now! All of you!' said Maqsud through gritted teeth and marched the children off.

Despondent, the three of them trudged home behind Maqsud's angry back. The prospect of going to the Urs seemed to be fading away very fast.

It was a silent dinner that night. Salim and Farida did not have much appetite anyway. After a while Maqsud said suddenly, 'How much did you earn today?'

'Ten annas and four paise. And we were selling at two paise per plate instead of one.' Farida, ever the businesswoman, replied, 'Double yesterday's price.'

'They were willing to pay extra for my singing,' said Salim.

'Singing? You call that singing?' Maqsud glared at his son.

'It'll pay for the sarai.'

There was a long, thoughtful silence. Then Maqsud said, 'Theek hai, you win. You can all stay the night at the Urs. I'll pay.' As they looked at him in surprise, a smile finally lit his face. 'But you must promise not to sell biryani again.'

'Of course!' said Salim in triumph. 'And can I sing in the chorus with you?'

'Nahin. You're still not good enough.'

'But his singing was good enough to sell two handis of biryani,' their mother commented dryly.

'I want a quawwal for a son,' Maqsud said firmly. 'Not a food shop owner.'

'Well, I tried!' sighed Salim inwardly. 'One day he'll give in and I'll sing at Nizamuddin.'

***

Finally it was the day they had been waiting for. It was the time of the Urs festival celebrated in memory of Amir Khusro, the famous poet, philosopher and historian, and a disciple of the saint Nizamuddin Auliya. Maqsud and his family travelled by bullock cart through the night and reached Nizamuddin as dawn was breaking.

All day, like curious visitors, they wandered through the bustling fair that had sprung up around the dargah of Nizamuddin, the tomb of the saint, and the Jamaat Khana mosque. Maqsud went in to say his prayers beside the hallowed mazaar of Nizamuddin Auliya, the great Sufi saint.

The place was full of pilgrims who had travelled for many days to attend the Urs. At the mazaar of Amir Khusro, they watched the pilgrims cover his tomb with beautifully embroidered chadars.

Salim hummed an Amir Khusro composition under his breath. Maqsud said to his son, 'You love Khusro's songs so much, do you know he is also said to have created the sitar?'

'Ji abbu,' Salim replied, very much in awe of the poet himself.

Farida wandered up to a secluded tomb which had grass growing on it and asked her mother, 'Why isn't this mazaar covered, ammi?'

'It's the resting place of Jahanara Begum, the daughter of Emperor Shahjahan. She was a poetess and wanted her tomb to be like those of the poor. Not covered in rich marble but simple, and open to the sky.'

As dusk fell, candles were lit and people started gathering to listen to "Dilli ke mahshoor quawwal" Maqsud Husain under a big tent. Even some of the noblemen from the court of Emperor Bahadur Shah Zafar were present.

From his corner Salim watched wistfully as his father put on the gold waistcoat and the fur cap. The men polished and tuned their instruments. Balle miyan drew the bow across the sarangi, Ram Pyare blew into his shehnai and Akhtar Khan tapped his tabla. Salim looked around the tent ... the air was electric with anticipation. He sighed.

Maqsud looked at his young son's solemn face and remembered his high sweet voice raised in song praising the biryani. He remembered how the people had smiled, and applauded. Salim had written the song and set it to music without any help. 'He's a performer too, my son Salim,' Maqsud thought.

'Salim!' he called.

'Ji abbu?' Salim came over. 'Shall I get your paan?'

'Yes. And then come up on stage with me.'

'Ji?' Salim couldn't believe his ears.

'You can sing in the chorus and clap. But very carefully. One wrong beat and I'll make you get off the stage.'

'Ji abbu!' Salim's face split into a huge grin.

Salim Husain, junior quawwal, adjusted the fur cap on his head, checked the buttons on the gold waistcoat and dusted down his kurta. Then he proudly walked up on stage behind his father. As he bowed low and greeted the audience, he saw his mother, Anwar and Farida in the front row, smiling widely. Then, sitting cross-legged in the chorus, he pushed back his sleeves to clap better, cleared his throat and was ready to sing.

Painting the Breeze

Parvati hummed as she worked. It was the first time in many days that she felt like singing.

For Parvati and her older brother Laxman, the last few days had not been easy. Their father lay ill, his body burning with fever. Even the herbs their mother had given him had not helped. The grain had finished and there was no money left either. Their father, after all, was just a potter, not a rich man. The only way out for Laxman was to make and sell the earthen pots and pans. He had worked with his father since he was a child but this was the first time they were on their own.

The brother and sister team had walked out of the gates of Pataliputra at dawn. The oil lamps in the niches of the tall wooden gates were dying and the watchmen dozing over their spears. Parvati and Laxman walked to the bank of the Ganga to collect clay. Then nervously they had shaped them into water pots and cooking bowls, lamps, vases and plates. Many broke, some were out of shape, a few cracked when fired in the kiln. But enough were left to sell, and yesterday they had bought rice and dal with their own earnings.

Today their father's fever had come down and there was food in the kitchen too. So Parvati sang as she worked, sitting at the edge of the courtyard near the lane which went past their little thatched hut.

Nobody had asked her to paint the pots but she knew painted pots sold better. All she had were the colours black and white that she made herself. She collected the soot from the lamps in the house, added oil to it and created her black colour. She ground some pieces of lime and mixed them with water to make the colour white. Her brushes were cotton pieces twisted to sharpen the edges. And with them she drew her dreams on the water pots and vases.

Everyone drew squares, triangles, straight and wavy lines. Parvati dipped the cotton into the white and thought, 'I don't want to draw just lines.'

She looked up at the sky and the clouds, cotton wool white after the rains. She drew a row of them around a pot, curved and floating like the smiles of the sky.

Pulling a plate closer, Parvati was startled by a red and black butterfly as it flew across her face and then fluttered down to perch on a yellow pumpkin flower on the courtyard hedge. And Parvati drew the curved wings with the tilted tips of the butterfly like a border around the plate.

The clatter of horse hooves, the clang of cowbells and the creak of a bullock cart made Parvati look up. Down their small dusty lane, a bullock cart came swaying. What made her sit up and watch was the rich cloth covering the cart, the bright curtains and the six horsemen riding behind the cart.

'A noble lady, I'm sure,' thought Parvati. She had seen a few drive by on the roads of Pataliputra. But she'd never seen a cart followed by six horsemen. By then Laxman had come to stand beside her.

'Look at the horsemen!' he exclaimed in admiration.

The horsemen were really a magnificent sight! Their short spears glittered in the sun. The saddlecloth on the horses were made of colourful cotton. Across their chest, over the sleeved tunic were the cross straps, to carry the quiver of arrows. The broad leather belt was for the sword and their headbands were tied across their foreheads with jaunty bows.

'Soldiers,' Laxman guessed. Then suddenly he ran back to the house, calling her. 'Parvati, come here!'

Parvati, reluctant to miss the spectacle, said, 'What?'

'Help me carry some of the pots outside.'

Working quickly, they lined up a row of pots along the lane and waited expectantly for the cavalcade to draw closer. When the bullock cart was within hearing distance, Laxman began to shout, 'Pots, O Noble Lady! Come and see our pottery!'

And Parvati joined in. 'Vases, incense holders, lamps! O Noble Lady!' Holding up the pottery and dancing with excitement, they made a huge din.

Suddenly, one of the horsemen rode up to them, lowered an angry moustached face and glared at them. 'Quiet! You impertinent fools! Don't you know who is in that cart?'

'No,' said Laxman. 'And how do you know the noble lady doesn't want to buy our pots?'

'Quiet!' growled the soldier. 'You move back now or I'll let my horse ride all over them.'

'Don't you dare!' Parvati stepped forward angrily. 'It took me all day to paint them.'

Before the soldier could do anything to the pots, a curtain was moved aside and a quiet voice said from inside the cart, 'One minute, soldier. I want to talk to these children.'

'Yes, my lady,' bowed the soldier, and turning his horse away, he rode back to join the other horsemen.

As Parvati and Laxman stood, tongue-tied, the voice said, 'Let's see your pots.'

Shyly they came closer as the curtain was swept back, and they saw the woman leaning against bolsters inside the cart, with a maid perched behind her. Laxman held out the pottery towards her. Parvati stood there, dazzled by what she saw. She had never seen anyone who looked so majestic before.

The lady's clothes were of the finest silk. The antariya, worn like a dhoti, was embroidered all over with gold. The uttariya, draped across her body like a dupatta, swept over her head. It was gossamer thin ,in a shade of dull gold, set with precious stones.

Parvati had seen noblewomen in the houses where they went to sell pottery, but never anyone who wore so much jewellery—the karnika, big gold earrings and the mekhala, a girdle round her waist made of silver chains. She wore two necklaces—the kantha, a short one of pearls, and the lambanam, a long gold chain, down to her waist. On her arms were thick kangans, bangles of gold, and the baju-bandh, an armlet on the upper arms that glittered with jewels. And her anklets were intricate designs in gold.

'And you, little girl,' the lady said briskly, breaking through Parvati's daze, 'where are the pots you were painting all morning?'

'I …' Parvati was suddenly overcome by shyness. 'I painted them for fun. You won't like them, my lady.'

'Show them to me, child,' the woman ordered gently.

Slowly Parvati pointed to the plate, the vase and the water pots before her. And then stood with bated breath as the lady turned them around to study the designs.

'I've never seen designs like these before,' she said thoughtfully. 'What were you drawing?'

'The sky,' said Parvati haltingly.

'Sky?' the woman laughed. 'How can you draw the sky?'

Parvati pointed to the clouds she had drawn around the water pot and said, 'If you draw clouds, what's around it becomes the sky.' Turning, she pointed to the palm tree at the corner of the courtyard. Its leafy fronds were swaying and bending. Then she said, 'That's the breeze.' The lady gave her a piercing look. 'And what's this?'

'Butterflies on the pumpkin flower.'

'And this?' she pointed to a vase with a curving design in black and white dots.

'That,' said Parvati, smiling, beginning to enjoy herself, 'is the koel's song from the bel tree.'

'A song. Of course!' the lady looked amused.

'Yes. It's like a waterfall of high and low notes.'

Carefully, the lady laid the pots inside the cart and then asked Laxman, 'How much do these cost?'

Laxman the businessman thought quickly. The lady was rich; she should be able to pay well. He thought as high as he could and said, 'Twelve panas. These are special pots, my lady.'

The lady and her maid hid a smile. 'Pay, Manjira,' she said. The maid, taking the copper pana coins out of a small bag tucked into her waist, paid Laxman.

'And you,' the lady touched Parvati's tousled head, 'whenever you draw the sky, the breeze or a song, child, bring the pots to my house. I will buy them all.' Then her eyes crinkled into a smile. 'I think my husband would like them too.'

'Where do you stay?' Parvati asked, and the maid laughed aloud.

The lady pointed to the soldiers who were all smiling, and said, 'Ask them. They will tell you the way.'

The curtain was swept back. As Parvati and Laxman stood watching, the bullock cart began to move again.

'Thank you, my lady,' they called out together.

The moustached horseman rode up and Laxman asked, 'Where does the lady stay, sir?'

The man's smile lingered. 'In the big palace with the carved wooden gates.' Then, noticing their puzzled faces, he laughed. 'That was our King Ashoka Vardhana's wife! Don't you recognise the

Queen when you see her? You two have just become potters to the royal family!'

Eyes wide with surprise, startled, hearts thudding, Laxman and Parvati turned to watch the convoy disappear in a haze of dust.

Dal Delight

Sadiq was sitting at his father's food shop in a small gali in Lucknow. He was swatting flies from a platter of biryani when he saw the man in a silk achkan get off a horse at their door.

'Looks rich—is he coming to our shop?' Sadiq wondered. Then he saw two servants fallowing him and thought, 'A nobleman, I'm sure!'

Sadiq's father Mohammad Qadir looked up from the kebabs he was frying on a huge angeethi, as one of the servants came to him in a hurry and said, 'Nawab Hasan Ali has come.'

The man in silk entered, and looking around their small shop, said in bored tones, 'I hear you are a famous cook, Mohammad Qadir. I like tasting new dishes and so I've come to your shop. 'What do you make best?'

'Dal,' said Sadiq's father, and went on frying the kebabs.

'Dal?' the nawab looked surprised. 'Only dal?'

'I can make biryani and korma and all the usual dishes, but you asked me what I cook best,' Qadir said calmly.

'But dal! That doesn't sound very exciting. My friends were praising your cooking so much, I expected something better.'

'But you haven't tasted the dal I make.'

'Fine, I'll taste it. What kind of dal do you prepare?'

'Urad.'

'Get me some. Let's see what's so special about it.'

'I haven't got it now.'

'What!' The nawab was looking angry. Sadiq felt worried.

'I make my dal shahi urad only when it has been ordered,' Qadir said. 'It takes me a day to make it, with a secret masala. If your honour so wishes, I'll have the dish prepared for tomorrow's lunch.'

'Alright,' Nawab Hasan Ali gave in. 'I live nearby. You can bring your dishes to my house tomorrow.'

'I'm sorry sir, that is not possible,' said Qadir. Sadiq sighed. His father was being difficult again.

His abbajaan lost lot of customers because he was such a fussy cook. And this nawab looked rich. They couldn't afford to lose him.

Nawab Hasan Ali had never met such a rude cook before but he was also beginning to be amused. 'What's the problem now, Qadir miyan?'

'Huzoor, to enjoy my dal you will have to come to my shop to eat it. It gets spoiled if it is taken off the angeethi. And your honour, once I call, you will have to come immediately.'

'Really? What if I'm late?'

'I'll throw the dal away or give it to the poor,' Qadir said as he slid some kebabs into the hot oil which landed with a hiss.

Nawab Hasan Ali shook his head. This Qadir was like no cook he had ever seen. *Ah well,* he thought, *let's taste his dal first. Maybe it will be worth the trouble.* 'Call me tomorrow when you're ready,' he said and left the shop.

Sadiq sighed in relief. He had been worried that the nawab would lose his temper and leave. Sadiq also knew that nawabs often gave big rewards to cooks if they liked a dish. His abbu had nearly spoiled everything. Sadiq was quite afraid of his father. When Mohammad Qadir became angry, the neighbours said, all the crows flew away cawing, and the street dogs hid behind trees. It was lucky the nawab was in a good mood and agreed to everything Qadir said. His father was quite capable of refusing to cook for the badshah himself if he wasn't treated right.

In the evening Sadiq went with his father to the market to buy all the ingredients for the dal shahi urad. Only the best would do, of course. The urad had to be perfect, each grain a pale ivory white, no broken bits, no stones or dust. Brown cinnamon sticks, cardamom, coriander, cumin and cloves, creamy-white garlic pods, onions, ginger and turmeric were to be ground and saffron and milk to be made into pure fragrant ghee. Green, crisp mint leaves would be needed for the chutney.

'Aadaab, Qadir miyan!' a man greeted them at the vegetable shop. 'How's the shopping going for dal shahi urad?' It was one of the servants who had accompanied Nawab Hasan Ali.

'Aadaab,' said Qadir shortly. He didn't like talking unnecessarily.

Sadiq smiled at the man and said, 'Your nawabsaab seems to like eating.'

'Ah! Does he!' the man laughed. 'It's his greatest hobby. He is always hunting for new food shops to try their cooking, and if he likes a particular preparation, he gives fabulous rewards.'

'Really?' Sadiq asked, excited. 'What rewards has he given?'

'Well, once he was so pleased by a pasanda and pulao in Aminabad, he bought the cook a new shop.'

'I can't believe it!' Sadiq exclaimed, wide-eyed. 'A whole shop!'

'The nawab is very rich. Last month he gave a diamond ring to a chef for his phirni.'

Qadir was calling him, so Sadiq had to leave, but all the way home he was dreaming of the reward his father could get. He knew his father's dal shahi urad tasted no less than any pulao or pasanda any cook could make.

Sadiq was at work with his father early next morning. He helped him clean the dal, make ghee, grind turmeric, peel and chop the onions, garlic and ginger. Then he watched Qadir cook the dal. The smell was mouth-watering. Qadir made a light cucumber raita, mint chutney on the side, a vegetable dish of cauliflower and potatoes and a plate of creamy, soft kakori kebabs. Once the nawab sat down to eat, he would serve freshly baked hot tandoori rotis. Finally, for dessert, there was phirni. Sadiq had sneaked a quick taste of the dal when his father wasn't looking; it tasted like nothing on earth. It was the secret masala that made the difference.

The time was right. The dal in the handi bubbled softly on the angeethi. The dough was ready to be slapped into rotis. The raita was cooling in an earthen bowl. Qadir turned to his son and said, 'Go call the nawab, beta. I'm ready to serve.'

Sadiq ran all the way to Nawab Hasan Ali's haveli. Panting, he reached the door of the house and told the servant, 'I've come to call nawabsaab for lunch. The dal is ready.'

'Ah! Yes, nawabsaab told me about that. Go up to the roof. He is flying kites there.'

Sadiq huffed up the stairs to the roof. The nawab and his friends were busy flying kites and were all excited about it. Sadiq went up to Hasan Ali and said timidly, 'Nawabsaab, the dal is ready. My father is calling you.'

Hasan Ali looked down at Sadiq and said, 'Who?' He then seemed to remember. 'Ah yes, the dal.'

One of his friends laughed. 'Forget the dal, Hasan. Your kite is in danger. That green one is about to cut it.

Hasan Ali hurriedly pulled his kite away, yelling, 'Just you wait, green kite! I'll get you.'

'Nawabsaab ...' Sadiq tried again, worried about his father's temper. 'The food is waiting.'

'Yes, yes,' he said, irritated. 'Tell your father to wait. Can't you see my kite is in danger?'

'Run along, boy,' one of the friends said impatiently. 'Can't you see nawabsaab is busy?'

'But the dal ...' and sadly, Sadiq gave up and slowly walked away. All his dreams were drifting away. He knew what would happen; he knew his abbu's temper. The moment Qadir heard that the nawab would rather fly kites than taste his dal, he would get into a flaming temper and give the handi of dal to the first beggar he would find.

Sadiq could forget about the reward. He felt like crying.

Slowly Sadiq walked home. He looked up to see the nawab's kite flying just overhead. Then he noticed his friend Aman flying a kite from his rooftop just across the lane. Sadiq got an idea.

He ran madly up the stairs to Aman and said, 'Aman, do something for me please!'

His friend looked back at him in surprise. 'What's the problem?'

'See that blue and silver kite? Cut it. Fast!'

'Sure. No problem!' Aman grinned. He was a champion at kite flying. He made a special kite string with a layer of ground glass on it that could cut through anything.

Sadiq raced back to the nawab's house, up the stairs, and reached the roof to see Aman get his kite's thread around the nawab's, give it a quick pull and ... 'Oh no!' Hasan Ali groaned in dismay as his kite swooped and fluttered towards the ground.

'Huzoor ...' Sadiq said, 'the food is waiting. The dal is delicious.'

'Oh yes, yes,' the nawab suddenly remembered. 'Now the kite's gone. Let us eat.'

The nawab and his friends walked with Sadiq. Nearing the shop, Sadiq raced ahead, his heart thumping nervously. 'Oh Allah,' he prayed, 'don't *let* abbu lose his temper. Please, don't let it be too late.'

'They are coming!' he yelled at his father. 'Abbu, is everything ready?'

'Yes,' muttered Qadir. 'What took you so long?'

The nawab and his friends entered the shop. The dastarkhwan was laid out in the best room. The food was served in the best silver bowls. As they sat down on the carpet, Qadir came in with the dal, and Sadiq followed with piping hot roti dripping with butter.

Nawab Hasan Ali broke a piece of roti, and as Sadiq watched breathlessly, dipped it in the dal shahi urad, put it in his mouth and chewed slowly. Then his eyes closed. 'Ah!' he said softly, and Sadiq let go of his breath.

The nawab dipped a second piece of roti in the dal, took a spot of raita with it, chewed and 'Ah!' he said louder. 'Qadir miyan, this dal shahi urad is straight from the heavens. I have never tasted anything better. Even a rogan josh pales before this.' His friends too were all exclaiming and praising the food with "wah wahs". 'You deserve a reward.' Hasan Ali continued. 'What would you like? Just ask.'

For the first time that day Mohammad Qadir smiled. 'I would like a better food shop, huzoor in a big market, near the imambara maybe.'

'Done!' said Hasan Ali, dipping into the vegetable and helping himself to a kakori kebab. He called one of his servants and waved at Qadir. The servant bowed low and put a bag full of money in Qadir's hand. 'It should be enough. If not, ask for more. Now give me some more of your dal shahi urad and a roti,' said Nawab Hasan Ali.

Sadiq sat and watched his father serve the guests. He found he was grinning to himself. Now they would be rich. Later, he would tell his abbu how he tricked the nawab into coming on time, by getting Aman to cut his kite. He knew his abbu would laugh and give him some money, maybe a whole mohur, and with it he and Aman would go to the market and buy kites and tops and eat kulfi and falooda.

Sadiq sat and smiled and kept smiling as Nawab Hasan Ali ate, and then ate some more.

Tenali Rama the Second

It was a cool, sunny morning in the city of Vijayanagar when the tall, dark man in spotless white cotton clothes strolled out of his house. Enjoying the beautiful day, he walked slowly towards the palace of King Krishna Deva Raya.

Past the orchards of a nobleman's mansion, he was walking under a stone gateway when he heard young voices raised in argument. The man stopped to listen.

'It's my turn to be Deva Raya … you promised!'

'Then can I be Minister Saluva Timma instead?'

Getting even more curious, the man peered past the gateway and first saw a plump boy with large bright eyes. As he flicked back his long hair, he said, 'Play any role you want as long as I am the royal court's wittiest and cleverest man … ahem …' He cleared his throat importantly. '… Tenali Rama, of course!'

With a silent laugh the man looked around, found a large boulder to sit on, and settled down. He was the only observer of the street show unfolding before him.

Half a dozen boys were acting out a day in the royal court of Vijayanagar. A sort of throne had been created using an old broken bed, covered with a tattered piece of matting. And now the boy playing Deva Raya strutted up importantly to his makeshift throne and sat down.

'Ah, Deva Raya!' sighed the observer with an inward grin as he noticed the boy's scuffed knees and bare feet. 'I wish you could see yourself now.'

The boys playing Tenali and Minister Timma stood on either side of the throne and the others playing courtiers stood before them. With a royal wave of a thin arm, the street side king yelled, 'Bring in the first case!'

A stocky boy came forward and said doubtfully, 'This is a real problem. Can you solve it?'

'Go on, Kesava.'

'I'm here about the cow, Your Highness,' said Kesava.

'Cow? What cow?' asked the puzzled prime minister Timma.

'His cow, my garden. What else?' Kesava looked impatient. The observer swallowed hard to stop himself from laughing out aloud.

'What cow? What garden?' Timma was beginning to sound a bit like a parrot.

'Explain yourself!' Deva Raya frowned regally.

'I mean my neighbour's cow getting into my garden,' Kesava was finally getting his words into some kind of order. Then the problem became clear.

The cow was always getting into poor Kesava's kitchen garden, chewing up the banana plants, devastating the pumpkin patch. And now trampling over the bamboo fence they had built, it had eaten his mother's precious marigolds. 'What can I do about it?'

Deva Raya frowned. 'Ask the neighbour to pay for the damages his cow has caused,' the twelve-year-old ended solemnly.

Kesava looked as solemn as Deva Raya as he said, 'I can't. My neighbour is a wrestler.'

'Oh!' the deflated faces proved the real problem was now finally being understood by the pavement king and his rag tag court. Deva Raya looked around helplessly at his ring of bedraggled courtiers and asked, 'What should Kesava do?'

The observer, forgetting about his errands of the morning, sat absorbed in the high drama. 'I have to ask the king,' he thought. 'What would he do to handle the wrestler and his heavyweight cow?'

The courtiers were coming up with solutions. 'Build a stone wall around the garden,' one suggested.

'Bah!' Kesava gave a dismissing shake of his head. 'You think my poor potter father has money for stone walls? He's still worried about the cost of the bamboo fence.'

'Then stop growing pumpkins,' said a thin boy with no front teeth.

'And what will my mother put in the sambaar?' asked Kesava. 'Grass?'

The observer, no longer able to stop himself, laughed out loud. Six pairs of astonished eyes looked at him.

'Forgive me, boys,' the man muttered. 'I hope you don't mind my listening to your problem. It's so interesting.'

'You're welcome, sir!' the half size Tenali Rama spoke for the first time, waving a pudgy hand. 'Maybe you have a solution?'

'Well …' the man scratched his chin thoughtfully. 'Kesava could send his goats to wreck the neighbour's garden.'

Kesava rolled his eyes in pure disgust. 'Devayya, dear Lord! You think my puny little goats have the courage to enter a garden guarded by a wrestler and his huge cow?'

'Then …' the man suggested apologetically, 'maybe you could refuse to let the cow go back?'

The chubby Tenali shook a tousled head. 'You're again forgetting the wrestler.' Then he gave a patient sigh. 'It looks like only I, Tenali, can solve this problem.'

'You can?'

'It's pretty simple really,' he sighed importantly. 'What do you like more, Kesava, pumpkin or payasam?' he asked suddenly.

'Payasam,' said Kesava promptly.

'Then the next time the cow is chewing the pumpkin vine, get a pot and quickly milk her. And give the milk to your mother to make payasam, or sell it to buy some pumpkin. Just see that the wrestler doesn't catch you stealing the milk,' Tenali shrugged disdainfully. 'Quite simple, don't you think?'

'Aah!' a satisfied sigh floated across the court. The problem had finally been solved.

The observer got up, walked up to Tenali and bowed low. 'Yes, you are truly as clever as the other Tenali and I feel you deserve this for solving a vexing problem.' And he gave the grinning boy a silver coin.

Leaving behind an excited bunch of boys planning what to buy with their sudden earnings, the real Tenali Rama walked away. Turning at the corner, he stopped and laughed in sheer delight. 'Well, Tenali,' he said to himself, 'you thought you were very clever. But a ten-year-old boy has beaten you.'

Then he hurried towards the palace. King Krishna Deva Raya would love this story!

A Shimmer of Silk

THAT morning Aditya did not come to beg at their house. Parvati had been waiting at the gate of the courtyard with the bowl of grain for a long time. The sun was climbing the sky, the lanes of Pataliputra were now busy with people, horses and bullock carts. Still Aditya did not come.

Aditya was much more than the Buddhist monk at the local monastery; he was their best friend. Every morning when the old bhikshu strolled up to their hut with his begging bowl, Parvati, her brother Laxman and their friend Nakul would gather around him. Aditya was a treasure house of stories—about the life of Gautama Buddha, and tales of distant lands. He even knew about how stars moved in the sky. But then, Aditya had this advantage—he knew how to read.

Laxman was helping his father at the potter's wheel. They made the beautiful black polished pottery that was typical of their city. While kneading the soft Ganga clay, he looked up and noticed Parvati's forlorn figure by the gate and walked over to her.

'What's happened to Aditya today? Usually he would have completed his rounds of begging by now.'

'Oh Laxman, I'm worried! Do you think he's ill? He's old, you know.'

'We'll go and check at the monastery,' Laxman said quickly, bending to wash his hands in a pot of water.

They hurried in through the high wooden gateway of the Buddhist vihara and immediately knew something was wrong. Usually the gardens around the monastery were tranquil with the call of birds, the air moving softly to the gentle chant of mantras intoned by the praying monks. Today clusters of saffron-clad monks stood anxiously whispering at the door of the prayer hall. There was no sound of bells and drums, no smell of incense. The still air was full of fear and dread.

They noticed a tall figure and ran to him.

'What's happened, Aditya?'

For the first time they saw Aditya's face without its calm smile. 'We have a situation here! There has been a theft, and Ananda, one of our oldest monks, has been injured.'

'A theft?' Laxman's eyes were wide with astonishment. 'Here?'

'Remember the jewelled box that the emperor had presented to the vihara?' the children nodded. 'We planned to place a relic of Lord Buddha in it. That box has been stolen. Ananda must have surprised the robbers in the prayer hall. He often comes to pray when he can't sleep. They hit him on the head and he's still unconscious,' Aditya sighed, distressed.

Parvati was thinking of the glittering ceremony at which their emperor Ashoka Vardhana, the beloved of the Gods, had presented the jewelled box to the vihara, at the inauguration of the new monastery.

It was one of the most beautiful viharas in Pataliputra, with a large prayer hall, its wooden pillars carved with holy Buddhist symbols like the lotus and the banyan tree. Ashoka had placed the box on a pedestal to the chanting of prayers and the spectators had sighed at the beauty of the box. Made of gold, inlaid with ivory, it was set with precious gems. Among them was the largest ruby in the kingdom. So precious, they could not even calculate its price in the gold nishka coins.

Parvati's reverie was broken by an anxious voice panting in her ear. 'Ha! Here you are. Everyone's wondering where you two had vanished.' And they turned to smile at their friend Nakul, who looked around and muttered, 'Looks like trouble.'

The three children had grown up together in the western end of Pataliputra where all the artisans and workmen lived. And like their emperor they were also Buddhists.

They turned at a stirring among the monks near the door of the monastery and then saw some of them carrying the old monk Ananda out carefully. They took him to the row of monk's cells and laid him down on a pallet in his tiny room. Watching from a window, the children saw Aditya clean the wound on Ananda's head and put a herbal balm on it. The old monk was still unconscious. Suddenly they saw Aditya stop and look closely at Ananda's clenched left hand. Bending closer, he prised open the fist and pulled out something. Covering Ananda with a blanket, Aditya left the room. Outside, Nakul ran up to Aditya. 'What did you find?'

Aditya showed them what he had in his hand. It was a torn piece of dark red cloth. 'Ananda must have clutched at the clothes of a robber and torn off a bit.'

First Nakul and then Laxman looked at the cloth. 'This is not enough to find the robbers.'

'Look carefully,' Aditya said.

Parvati took the fragment and softly rubbed it between her fingers. 'It's soft!' she exclaimed. 'Much softer than the cloth we wear.'

'It's silk,' Aditya said, 'not cotton.'

Parvati looked even closer. 'And it has something woven in gold in it.' Being a potter's daughter, she even noticed the design. 'It's very different from the patterns we use in Pataliputra.'

By now all of them were bent over the fragment of silk. A jaggedly torn piece, probably from a turban, it shimmered in Parvati's hand and the geometric design in gold glittered against the dark red ground. 'Maybe the silk is from some other land.'

'You mean the robbers were foreigners?'

'Or someone bought it from them.'

'But how will you find out where the cloth came from?' Aditya asked gently. They looked at him in silence. 'A potter knows all about pottery,' Aditya prompted.

'Of course!' Laxman said excitedly. 'We'll go and ask a weaver. He'll know where such silk is woven,' and in a moment the three of them had rushed out of the monastery.

Going past the wooden palaces of the noblemen, zigzagging through the busy streets, they finally reached the cluster of thatched huts where the weavers lived. It is easy to find the weavers because from far away you can hear the "click clack" of their looms.

Bending low, they entered a hut and walked up to a man bent over a loom. The weaver looked up. 'Yes?'

'We need your help, sir,' Laxman said politely, pulling out the piece of silk. 'Could you tell us where we can find cloth like this?'

'Why do you want to know?' the man asked curiously as he fingered the silk.

'We work at a nobleman's house,' Parvati stepped in quickly, making up a story. 'Our mistress wants silk like this for her uttariya.'

'We don't make this here. You'll have to buy it from the traders. This silk is woven in a land in the east, many months' journey across the snowy mountains.'

'How do you find these traders?'

'When they come here, they set up camp near the eastern gate. Though I must warn you, this silk will cost your mistress many silver dharana coins.'

The three of them walked back to the monastery to tell Aditya what they had found out. Then they wandered homeward tiredly. It was late afternoon and they were hungry. The search for the silk traders would have to wait for the next day. While eating a late lunch, Parvati wondered, 'How do we find out about the silk? Would the traders expect us to buy some?'

'You'll have to make up another story to avoid that,' laughed Nakul.

Next morning after an early lunch of rice and vegetables the three of them began the long walk towards the eastern gate. They wore their best dresses hoping the traders would take them to be rich enough to answer their questions. The antariyas the boys wore, tied like dhotis, were made of fine cotton, while the uttariya, they had draped like a shawl over it, was woven with a bright pattern. Parvati wore her antariya like a long skirt, in pretty flowered muslin, and she had tied a bright kayabandh at the waist.

They took the road going past the tall walls of the city. Pataliputra was surrounded by wooden walls to protect it from invaders. The walls were so high that no enemy could ride over them. The city could be entered by the four main gates, which were guarded day and night. Around each gate there were niches carved in the walls where small ghee lamps were lit at night to guide the travellers.

At the eastern gate the traders' camp was visible from far off. It was a cluster of bright tents busy with people, the call of traders and the hum of business. They wandered around, their eyes wide with astonishment at all the fantastic things from faraway lands that were being sold. Exotic jewels and rolls of many-hued cloth, carved wood, leather and ivory, incense, perfumes and spices, herbs and magic potions to cure all illnesses.

Suddenly Parvati pointed excitedly. In one of the smaller tents, a man sat before bales of cloth and they all had that unmistakable shimmer of silk. They stood watching the man, wondering what to do next. 'How do we ask him about the silk without him getting suspicious?' Laxman wondered.

Then something made them stop and watch. The trader, a tall muscular man in a silk antariya and a stitched tunic suddenly stood up, looked around himself carefully and then nodded mysteriously.

'Quick! Hide!' Nakul said urgently, and in a moment they had slipped to the side of the tent and crawled through an opening to a spot from where they could look past the bales of cloth. Finding a gap, they peered in to see the trader standing in a hidden corner, waiting.

Another man came hurrying in and said, 'Shilaka?' The trader nodded. 'The message for you is—listen carefully—the treasure chest of the Sakya prince will await you at nightfall on Tuesday where the oars first touch the river. Beware! The monks are powerful and the king is angry.'

Shilaka, the trader, thought for a moment and then said, 'I understand.' Then, handing a coin to the man, he said, 'Thank you. Tell him I'll be there.' Having said his bit, the second man walked away.

The three children crept out of their hiding place and quickly walked away. 'I didn't understand the message at all!' Nakul said, puzzled. 'Except for the last bit.'

'Let's go and tell Aditya,' Laxman suggested. 'He's good at solving riddles.' They hurried towards the monastery.

They rushed into Aditya's cell in the monastery but it was empty. A monk came in and they asked him where Aditya was. 'He was with Ananda, tending to his wounds,' the monk told them.

Ananda was alone. He lay still on his pallet but his eyes were open. Hearing their footsteps, he turned to look at them.

'Ananda, do you know where Aditya is?' Parvati asked anxiously.

'He's gone to meet the king,' Ananda said slowly. 'To tell Ashoka Vardhana of the theft.'

'When will he be back?'

'Tomorrow maybe. He left last evening.'

'Oh no!' Nakul said. As they left Ananda and went into the monastery garden, Nakul turned to the others. 'Now what do we do?'

'Solve the riddle ourselves,' Parvati said firmly. She continued softly, 'The treasure chest of the Sakya prince ...'

Parvati had an amazing memory. She never forgot what she heard and now she repeated the exact words the man had whispered to Shilaka. '... will await you at nightfall on Tuesday. Where the oars first touch the river.'

Sitting down under a shady peepal tree, they pondered over the words. 'Sakya prince?' Nakul muttered. 'Who's a Sakya prince? Our king is a Mauryan.' Then his eyes went to the carved walls of the monastery and his face brightened with excitement, 'Of course! Gautama Buddha! Aditya told us he was a Sakya prince and ...'

'... the treasure chest is the jewel box in which his relic was to be kept!' Laxman completed his words.

'At nightfall on Tuesday,' Parvati's eyes widened in panic. 'But that's tonight!'

'But where are they planning to meet?'

'Where oars touch the river?' Nakul frowned. 'Oars touch the river everywhere.'

'Oars first touch ...' Parvati corrected him, '... where the boatmen first dip their oars into the water, and that is at ...'

'The ghat!' The three of them sprang up in excitement. 'They plan to meet at the Ganga ghat from where the boats cross the river. Let's go!'

As they hurried towards the gate of the monastery, Laxman stopped. 'Wait! We'll need help.' And turning back, he ran to Ananda and quickly told him of their discovery.

Ananda's eyes blazed with anger. 'They will not be allowed to get away! You three go to the ghat. I'll send a message to Aditya at the palace right now.'

As they hurried towards the ghat, Laxman said, 'You know, if I could read and write like the monks, I would have sent the message to Aditya myself.'

'Who's heard of a potter's son who can read?' Nakul laughed.

By now they had walked out of the gate of Pataliputra and reached the bank of the Ganga river. The sun was sinking, flecking the ripples in the river with gold. Looking around, they saw an old boat lying upturned by the ghat and hid behind it to wait.

Time passed slowly. A cool evening breeze blew in from the river as night fell. The boatmen tied their boats up and went home. Slowly the place fell silent. As Laxman slapped angrily at a mosquito, Parvati whispered, 'Shh! I can hear someone.'

Carefully they peered from behind the boat and saw the shadowy figure of a horseman ride slowly to the ghat. Getting off, the man tied the horse to a shrub. Then he walked closer to the river and stood waiting. Looking hard in the gloom, Nakul said, 'I think it's Shilaka, the trader.'

A few minutes later they saw another figure come walking towards Shilaka. This man was carrying a large bundle in his arms. Shilaka walked forward to meet him.

'What do we do now?' Parvati asked anxiously. 'Aditya hasn't come with the soldiers.'

'We'll stop them somehow,' Laxman said, springing up from behind the boat. 'Follow me!'

The second man was handing the bundle to Shilaka when three small shadows came streaking towards them. 'Hey! Wha...' yelled Shilaka as Parvati snatched the bundle from his hands and ran, while Laxman and Nakul jumped on the men with loud yells, punching and scratching like two angry cats.

They fought as hard as they could but the two men were much too strong for the boys, who were pushed to the ground. And soon the men were chasing Parvati. The boys scrambled up and ran after them because somehow Parvati had to be defended.

By then Shilaka had caught up with Parvati and clutching her arm, he whirled her around. They all stopped and stared in surprise. Parvati's hands were empty!

'Where's the box?' Shilaka yelled. 'Tell me or I'll break your arm!'

Parvati stood there, her face mutinous—a tiny, brave figure. She blinked and said, 'What box?' Just then Nakul and Laxman reached the men and attacked them again.

They were about to get beaten again when they all heard the sound of horses galloping towards them and Aditya's voice calling, 'Laxman! Parvati! Nakul!' The king's men had arrived.

Knowing their game was up, the two men turned to flee, but the boys dived to grab their legs. The men fell, scrambled up and turned to run again, but being at the edge of the river, and the ground being muddy and slippery, they fell again. By then the soldiers carrying spears and flaming torches had surrounded them. Aditya sprang down from his horse and ran up to the children, hugging them in relief. 'Oh thank the lord you are safe! I was worried I'd be too late.'

Shilaka and the thief of the box stood before them, their hands tied. Aditya took a closer look at the second man and said in surprise, 'Vamana, you?' And then turning to the captain of the soldiers, he said, 'This man used to work in the monastery. He helped us in building cells for monks.'

The children noticed Vamana's clothes. He wore a silk antariya woven with unusual gold patterns—just like the fabric Shilaka was selling. Obviously Vamana planned to sell the box to a trader who would take it to some other land to get a high price for it.

'But where is the box?' Aditya asked, puzzled. With a quick laugh, Parvati ran to the bush where Shilaka had tied his horse, and from behind it, brought out the wrapped bundle.

'I knew Shilaka would never think of looking near his own horse!' she giggled.

Aditya laughed in delight. 'Clever Parvati!'

Opening the bundle carefully, Aditya brought out the beautiful relic box as they all gathered around to admire it. The gold gleamed, and the large stone on the lid glowed in the light of the torches. Aditya smiled gratefully at them. 'You three deserve a reward for such bravery and cleverness. What would you like?'

'Well, there is one thing ...' Laxman began.

'Will you teach us to read and write?' Nakul completed his words.

'So that I can read our legends,' Laxman said dreamily.

'And I could write poetry,' added Parvati.

Looking at their dusty faces, Aditya laughed. Nakul was sporting a big bruise. Laxman had a black eye. 'Trust you three to ask for such an uncommon reward! Of course I'd love to teach you.'

Hasan and the Lost Pigeons

'Abbu, where are Resham and Badal?' Hasan called out to his father anxiously. 'They are not in their pigeon house!'

'What!' Nasir miyan came running, and the two of them searched everywhere, among the pigeon houses and cages. The famous pair of gerobaaz pigeons, Resham and Badal, were nowhere to be found.

Hasan was a pigeon person like his father, who was the kabutarbaaz, the pigeon expert, at the house of Nawab Sajjad Ali of Lucknow. Nasir miyan cared for and trained the pigeons that the nawab kept as pets. He had over a hundred of them, but the most beautiful were the gerobaaz pair of Resham and Badal. The pigeons, both lovely, pale grey-white in colour, had been brought from far off Kabul in Afghanistan, and now they were missing.

Early that morning, like every day, Hasan had gone to the back garden of the beautiful haveli of the nawab in Hazratganj. He had cleaned the pigeon houses and cages, changed the water in the drinking bowls and added fresh bird feed in the bowls. As he worked, Hasan also talked to the pigeons. They were his friends.

The pair of tiny goli kabutars had come out busily to peck grain from his hand. The lotan kabutars sat all puffed up, muttering and cooing to each other. But when he came to Resham and Badal's pigeon house, it was empty. His heart thudding with worry, Hasan ran to call his father. Then he went in to tell Nawab Sajjad Ali.

'It has to be that thief Maqbool Ali,' said the nawab, huffing angrily. 'He has always wanted my gerobaaz pigeons. I'm sure he's stolen them.'

'But how can that be possible, huzoor?' Nasir miyan protested. 'He is a nawab. He wouldn't steal.'

'Of course he could. He may not have come himself. He's too fat, poor man, to do that, but someone stole my gerobaaz for him.'

The two nawabs, Sajjad Ali and Maqbool Ali, were old rivals. Both kept pigeons as pets and they were always trying to get the better of the other. When Resham and Badal arrived, the stories of their beauty and intelligence brought all the pigeon lovers flocking to Sajjad Ali's house, and Maqbool Ali felt he was losing the fight.

Resham and Badal were beautiful and faithful. Hasan loved them. Every morning Nasir miyan would let them out and they would fly around the haveli all day. Sometimes Hasan would sit by the stone lily pool in the garden and watch the shadow of the two pigeons streak back and forth across the water. All Nasir miyan or Hasan had to do was whistle, and the pigeons would flutter down to sit on their shoulders.

'What do we do, huzoor?' Nasir miyan asked the nawab.

'I'll send some men to find where that Maqbool Ali has hidden them.'

'You'll have to hurry,' Nasir miyan said. 'I'm worried they may cut the pigeon's wings—it is the only way to keep them from flying home.'

'But who do I send?' the nawab pondered.

'Huzoor,' Hasan said softly, 'let me go. I know the house. My friend Salim works there. I think he can help.'

'Go, beta, run!' the nawab said, 'while I get some others to follow. I pray they haven't cut the wings.'

Hasan ran all the way to his friend's house and entered, yelling, 'Salim! Salim!'

'Arrey! What's the matter?' Salim came out munching his breakfast.

'You have to help me. Abbu and I are in real trouble.'

'Why? What happened?'

'Resham and Badal have been stolen and the nawab thinks Maqbool Ali's men must have stolen them.'

'What do we do now?' Salim asked. 'I could look around when I go to work at Maqbool Ali's house.'

'I have a better plan. Take me with you. Say that I need a job, and when I find Resham and Badal I'll try to steal them back. Can you do it?'

Salim nodded, a shade doubtfully.

The two boys walked to Nawab Maqbool Ali's house in Nazirabad. As they entered, Salim said, 'What kind of job should I say you'll do?'

'What do you do?'

'Oh, I hover around the nawabsaab's room and run his errands—get him paan, freshen his hookah, that sort of thing. I help the nawab's personal khansama too.'

'Well,' Hasan said thoughtfully, 'the only thing I can really do is take care of pigeons.'

A thin old khansama stood at the door of the nawab's room. He glared at Salim and said, 'You're late again.'

'I'm sorry bhaijaan,' Salim apologised, 'but my friend has come from the village and he needs a job. So I brought him to you.'

'What can you do?'

'He's very good with animals,' Salim said quickly, 'and birds.'

The khansama was thoughtful. 'Nawabsaab was saying this morning that he needs an extra hand to take care of the pigeons. He's got some new ones yesterday.'

Hasan's heart raced when he heard that. 'I can work with pigeons, huzoor,' he said anxiously.

'Wait here.' The khansama went in. Coming out again, he beckoned to them to follow him.

Nawab Maqbool Ali was a huge, fat man. He sat on a couch, leaning against a large bolster, his mouth full of paan, and a hookah near his hand. Beside him on a table stood a beautiful cage with two grey-white pigeons in it.

'It's Resham and Badal!' Hasan whispered excitedly.

'Shut up!' Salim said fiercely.

Maqbool Ali looked up at Hasan and said, 'You take care of birds?'

'Huzoor,' Hasan bowed his head.

'Understand pigeons?'

'Ji.'

'Where did you learn?'

'At my village, huzoor,' Hasan made up a story quickly. 'I met an old baterbaaz and he taught me to take care of birds. I worked with him for a year.'

'Well, my kabutarbaaz needs an assistant. I bought a lot of pigeons yesterday. Can you work with him?'

'Ji,' said Hasan, and glancing at Resham and Badal, thought, 'I'll steal back my pigeons too.'

Salim took Hasan to the pigeon house in the rear courtyard. The kabutarbaaz was a bad-tempered man in his red fez cap with its tassel, and a beard reddened with henna. He looked glumly at Hasan and then growled, 'Ha! Ask for an assistant and nawabsaab sends me a child.'

'He's very good, miyan,' Salim said soothingly.

'That's what you say because he's your friend,' the kabutarbaaz said. 'But what can a small boy know about pigeons?'

'I can show you,' Hasan said. 'Do you have any lotan kabutars?'

The kabutarbaaz pointed to a cage and said, 'There!'

Hasan stood by the lotan pigeons, stroking them and talking to them, making friends. Then he threw the pigeons into the air. They fluttered and circled above him and when he whistled, they came and settled on his shoulders.

'That,' the kabutarbaaz dismissed, 'is very easy

to do. Any boy who keeps birds can teach them to do that.'

Hasan smiled. He flew the pigeons again and now made them fly in circles above his head by just waving a handkerchief. Then, as Hasan and Salim stood with grain in their hands, Hasan whistled. The pigeons flew straight to him to peck the grain.

'Achcha ...' the kabutarbaaz said reluctantly. 'You know some things, but you'll have to learn more and work very hard.'

'Ji,' said Hasan politely.

Working at the pigeon cages, Hasan worried about how he was going to steal Resham and Badal. In the afternoon as he sat eating his lunch with Salim, he said, 'What do I do? The nawab has been sitting with Resham and Badal all morning. How do I steal them?'

Salim looked thoughtful. 'I'll find a way.'

Later in the day, Hasan was sitting in the garden when he saw Salim waving frantically from the house. He ran to him.

'Quick!' Salim said urgently. 'I just saw nawabsaab leave the sitting room. I think he's gone for a nap, and the khansama's gone too. He called me to help him with the hookah.

'You go in,' said Salim and quickly walked away.

Looking around carefully, Hasan slipped into Maqbool Ali's room. He went to the table where

Resham and Badal sat in their cage, but as he tried to pick it up he found that it was chained to the table. Talking softly to the pigeons, Hasan opened the cage and gently took them out. Recognizing his voice, Resham and Badal came strutting out and then fluttered up to sit on his shoulders.

Hasan stood stroking the birds and talking to them. He loved them. It was so good to have them back. Badal pecked at his hair. Their feathers were soft as silk and the colour of clouds. That's why he had named them Resham and Badal—silk and cloud.

Hasan turned towards the door, planning to get out quickly, with the pigeons still perched on his shoulders, but froze in surprise. On the threshold, his huge body leaning on a stick, Nawab Maqbool Ali stood looking coldly at him.

'What do you think you are doing with my gerobaaz?' Maqbool Ali asked, his voice icy with anger.

'Huzoor ...' Hasan said nervously, 'I was just ...'

'Who let you enter my room?' Maqbool Ali thundered.

'I wanted to see your gerobaaz, huzoor,' Hasan said quickly. 'They are so beautiful. I came in to give them grain.'

'Put them back in the cage,' the nawab yelled, frightening Hasan even more. 'Immediately!' And then he called out, 'Khansama!'

As Hasan sadly put Resham and Badal back into the cage, the old khansama came running. 'What's the matter?' he panted.

'This boy took my gerobaaz out of their cage,' Maqbool Ali shouted. 'He may be a thief. Kick him out of the house. I never want to see his face again.'

So, out of a job within hours, Hasan walked tiredly home, feeling sad and very disappointed. 'Oh Allah,' he thought sadly, 'it all went wrong. What do I do now?' Slowly Hasan headed for Sajjad Ali's haveli.

'Are you sure they are our pair?' Sajjad Ali asked Hasan, back in the haveli.

'Ji, I know Resham and Badal. Resham had lost some feathers of her right wing and that is how I recognised her.'

'Have they cut the wings?' Nasir miyan asked anxiously.

'No abbu, I think the nawab does not know they are stolen. He bought a lot of pigeons yesterday and he thinks the pair has been bought for him from Kabul.'

'Well, we'll see tomorrow,' Sajjad Ali said thoughtfully. 'I think we will visit Maqbool Ali and see for ourselves.'

Early next morning Sajjad Ali, Nasir miyan and Hasan reached Maqbool Ali's haveli. If the nawab was surprised to see his rival, he didn't show it. Bowing slightly, he gave a crooked smile and said, 'Welcome, nawabsaab! What a pleasant surprise so early in the morning. Have you come to see my new gerobaaz pair? Come in! Come in!'

As they went in, Hasan saw Salim and the khansama looking at them in surprise from the door of the sitting room. Just then Maqbool Ali noticed Hasan and growled, 'What is this boy doing here? I ordered him to leave.'

'He is with me, nawabsaab,' Sajjad Ali said. 'And I haven't come to see your gerobaaz pair. I've come to take them back.'

'What!' Maqbool Ali exclaimed in surprise.

'My pair was stolen and sold to you.'

'Nonsense. Do you think I'm a fool to pay a thousand rupees for your pair?'

'You have been cheated. They are my pair, Resham and Badal. This boy ...' Sajjad Ali pointed to Hasan, '... he is the son of my kabutarbaaz and he takes care of them. He recognised the pigeons yesterday.'

Maqbool Ali gave Hasan a dirty look. 'Aha! Now I understand your plan. You sent this boy to my house to steal my gerobaaz and when he failed, you've come up with this story.'

'Now look here, Maqbool Ali. Will you ...'

'I don't want to talk about it.' Maqbool Ali was red in the face with anger. 'The gerobaaz pair is mine!' He turned to enter the sitting room followed by Sajjad Ali and the others.

On the table, Resham and Badal still stalked the cage. Nasir miyan took one look at them and said, 'Huzoor, these are our birds.'

'Of course you'll say that,' Maqbool Ali said. 'I won't let you take my birds just because someone stole your pair.'

'Maqbool Ali, don't be a fool!' Sajjad Ali had also lost his temper now. 'Do you think I would lie to you?'

'I beg your pardon!' Maqbool Ali said coldly. 'I think this argument has gone on long enough. I would be grateful if you and your men would kindly leave.'

'Now what do I do?' Hasan thought. He looked anxiously at Salim who was standing near the door. To his surprise, Salim was behaving very oddly. He gave a quick shake of his head towards the pigeon cage and suddenly Hasan heard him yelling, 'Nawabsaab! They're stealing the pigeons! Stop! Thief!'

In a flash Maqbool Ali had rushed out of the room towards the garden followed by his servants. Sajjad Ali and Nasir miyan were looking at each other in surprise at the sudden excitement when Hasan quickly sprung into action. He ran to the cage, opened it, took Resham and Badal to the window and threw them high up into the air. The pigeons fluttered around in the sky, a little confused, and then flew off.

Leaving everyone still rushing around in the house and garden looking for thieves, Hasan and Salim ran out of the haveli trying to follow the two pigeons.

'Don't worry!' Hasan laughed happily, 'They'll go home.'

By the time Salim and Hasan reached the pigeon houses at Sajjad Ali's haveli, Resham and Badal had been home a long while and had settled down. Resham sat in a round ball of feathers, beak tucked in, asleep. Badal was at the bowl of bird feed.

The two nawabs followed by their servants came hurrying in. Sajjad Ali pointed triumphantly at the pigeons and said, 'See! They flew straight back to their nest. If they were not mine, would they have come to my house?'

'Ah well,' Maqbool Ali emitted a sigh of defeat. 'You are right. Pigeons do fly home and these are your pigeons. It looks like I was fooled.' He called out to his servants. 'Roshan! Ali! Sardar! Find the thief who cheated me. Immediately. I want my money back. I am very upset!'

Sajjad Ali patted his arm sympathetically. Then, he asked Maqbool Ali, 'Nawabsaab, do you think you could accept a little present from me?'

'Of course.'

Sajjad Ali went to one of the pigeon cages and came back with a pair of white pigeons. 'This is a very good shirazi pair. They haven't been trained yet and will be happy in your home.'

'Bahut shukriya! Thank you nawabsaab!'

Watching Maqbool Ali leave, Salim said, 'Well, you've got your pigeons back but helping Hasan to free them, I may have lost my job.'

Nawab Sajjad Ali smiled. 'Never mind. You are most welcome at my house. You can work here with your friend Hasan, my chhota kabutarbaaz. Here's a mohur for each of you for being so clever. From now on, Resham and Badal are in Hasan's special care. They are really your pigeons. Look after them well.'

'Ji huzoor!' Hasan and Salim said happily, as Resham and Badal flew down to patter around Hasan's feet.

No Pulao for Nawabsaab

Nawab Bashir Khan glared at his cook Ishaq and yelled, 'It's all your fault!'

Ishaq strode silently before him, but his round, fair face was beginning to flush with anger.

'You don't care about my health.' Nawabsaab had already lost his temper. 'You don't even know how to cook well ...'

'What!' Ishaq's eyes widened in surprise. 'This has nothing to do with my cooking.'

'Really?'

'Of course. I'm a great cook—everyone says so. But the person eating what I cook has to know when to stop.'

'You mean ...' Nawabsaab was so stunned at Ishaq's reply, he could only gulp and stare in surprise.

'Yes. It's all because huzoor does not control his eating.'

'How dare you! And who says you are a great cook? You're just as bad as some roti-slinger from a food shop in the Chowk!' And then nawabsaab stopped, with a feeling that he had gone too far. Trying to look nonchalant, he sat back on his takht, leaned against a bolster, and picked up his hookah.

There was a long tense silence as his words seemed to slowly sink into Ishaq's mind and made him swell with indignation before the nawab's eyes. Ishaq took a deep breath and then said through gritted teeth, 'We have been personal bawarchis to nawabs for six generations. If huzoor does not like my cooking, it is his misfortune. I will leave immediately for Aligarh.'

'Aligarh?'

'The great amir, Nawab Asafjah, has often invited me to take over his kitchen. Now I will do so.'

With this parting shot, Ishaq swivelled on his heels and stalked out of the baithak, leaving the speechless nawab holding his hookah and staring after him. Behind a door, two boys had been listening all the while. Aslam turned to Javed and said, 'Aligarh? I don't want to go to Aligarh.'

In the city of Dilli, there were many famous and rich noblemen. And in comparison, Nawab

Bashir Khan was just a small nawab. It's true, compared to the others, his haveli in Daryaganj was a small house. There were only a few horses in the stables and only a dozen pet pigeons in the rooftop birdhouse. But he had one thing envied by many—his cook, Ishaq.

Nawabsaab loved to entertain, and no one ever refused an invitation to a meal cooked by Ishaq. Every meal would come with delicious surprises—a unique biryani or a specially flavoured kebab. And now Ishaq was going to Aligarh!

Aslam was Ishaq's son. His friend Javed's father was the nawab's manager. His job involved running the house and farm, and supervising the stables. The two boys had grown up together and were beginning to help their fathers around the haveli. One day Aslam would rule over the kitchen and Javed would step into his father's shoes. And the two friends would always be together. That is, if Aslam did not go to Aligarh.

Actually, it had all begun with nawabsaab's horse. That morning, nawabsaab had planned to visit a friend in Chandni Chowk and Javed's father waited at the door with his horse. Nawabsaab came out and was about to get on the horse when it whinnied and backed away nervously. He tried again and once more the horse moved.

'What's the matter with him?'

Javed's father bit his lip and then said, 'Huzoor, will you promise not to get angry?'

'I won't—now what's the matter?'

'Well, this horse is very old and you've become too heavy for him. Maybe we could get a ...'

With his face swelling in anger, nawabsaab cancelled his trip and walked quickly towards his baithak. By the time he reached it, he was very short of breath, sweating, and his heart was thudding so hard that Javed had to run and call the hakim.

The hakim checked the nawab's pulse, stared into his eyes, made him cough and tapped his chest. He cleared his throat and said, 'It's nothing serious—yet.' He asked to speak to nawabsaab's wife, the begum sahiba.

The chick curtains were lowered on one side of the room and begum sahiba came and stood behind it to listen to Hakimji. 'Your husband, begum,' said the old man, 'is grossly overweight. I've warned him before, but he does not listen. Now you have to do something.'

'He will listen to me.' Begum sahiba's firm voice came from behind the curtain.

'Bahut achcha—see that he only eats dry rotis and light vegetables. No ghee, little meat or wine. And make him take long walks every morning.'

'Ji,' said the begum calmly.

No rogan josh! No pulao! Long walks! Everyone had been saying such awful things to nawabsaab.

Sitting there he got angrier and angrier, and he took it all out on poor Ishaq. And Ishaq lost his temper and quit.

Something had to be done. And quickly. Ishaq had already ordered Aslam and his mother to start packing. They were to leave the day after.

The two friends sat and worried about it.

'We could try talking to nawabsaab,' Javed said.

'Won't work. He's still too angry. At begum sahiba's orders abbu served him boiled spinach and rotis for lunch.'

'Could we persuade Ishaq chacha, then?'

'Abbu? Impossible! He says tomorrow he'll make plain dal and roasted brinjal for dinner, and then quit.'

'We have only tomorrow to do something!' Javed said dejectedly.

Next morning, a very glum nawabsaab began his morning walk. What was more insulting was that begum sahiba had made the boys accompany him to make sure that he walked and did not waste time chatting with people on the way.

Since the house was quite close to the river, they decided to stroll along the banks of the Jamuna. It was cool and quiet that summer morning. A few washermen slapped clothes on large stones. Boats carrying vegetable and grain into the city floated by. As they went past a patch of ripening watermelons, Javed said, 'These tarbuz are nearly ripe.'

Nawabsaab sighed. 'Ah! But will that cruel hakim let me eat them?'

'Of course!' said Aslam. 'Abbu will make a light sherbet flavoured with mint leaves and ...' he stopped.

There was a small silence and then the nawab sighed, 'But he'll be in Aligarh!'

The boys exchanged a quick glance and then Aslam said carefully, 'If huzoor spoke to him, abbu would stay.'

'Never! Your father was very rude to me. And I've known him for 20 years.'

They walked on in silence. At a ghat below the walls of the Red Fort, a boat was unloading baskets of vegetables. Javed said, 'Look at those pumpkins! Just what Ishaq chacha likes to use for his tari wali sabji.'

'You forget he'll be in Aligarh,' said nawabsaab in a small voice.

As if he hadn't heard the nawab, Aslam joined in. 'And then the lightly spiced pasanda, and with it a dry chutney with raisins and raw mangoes, don't you think?'

The nawab only sighed, and the boys finally gave up. It looked like Aslam would have to go to Aligarh, after all.

At the haveli gates, nawabsaab mused, 'The walk's made me hungry. Wonder what Ishaq's made for breakfast.' And then he glanced at the solemn faces of the two boys, squared his shoulders and said, 'Okay, I'll talk to him.'

Ishaq was in the kitchen. Nawabsaab walked up to him and said, 'Ishaq! I order you to stay!'

Ishaq stood up, looked stonily into the distance and silently shook his head. 'Oh no!' thought Aslam in panic. 'Now abbu's being difficult.'

'Why not?' thundered the nawab.

'I'm not a roti-slinger. I'm an artist and I work where my talents are appreciated.'

With a quick look at the boys' anxious faces, the nawab decided to sound milder. 'Look, we both got angry yesterday. Let's forget it. We've been together for years!'

But Ishaq stood stubbornly silent. Aslam was so disappointed, he was close to tears. A very sad nawab was turning away when Javed piped up, 'And what about your grand banquet next month, huzoor?'

'What about it?'

'The greatest nawabs, omrah and amirs of the court of our emperor, Shah Alam, will be coming …'

'Oh, it's all planned. I'll get Kashmiri basmati rice,' the nawab said dreamily, 'and tender mutton. Fresh rohu fish from the river and the choicest vegetables. Zafran and the best Dusheri mangoes from Malihabad.' Without thinking, Ishaq added just as dreamily, 'I've already planned the menu. We'll begin with a shorba of …'

'But you'll be in Aligarh!' shouted nawabsaab and the boys.

Ishaq looked at the three laughing faces and then his face cracked into a smile. 'No. I'll be right here, cooking that banquet.'

The boys did a little dance of delight behind nawabsaab's huge back. Aslam could stay with his best friend Javed in Dilli!

'Good,' said nawabsaab, walking out of the kitchen. 'What's for lunch?'

'Urad dal, lauki ki sabji and roti, at begum sahiba's orders.'

'No meat?' Nawabsaab's voice began to rise, and then he checked himself. 'Fine. I'll be good. Light food, long walks and no pulao. But Ishaq, on banquet night, I'll eat as much as I want and no one will stop me.'

'Ji huzoor,' said Ishaq.

'Shall I serve breakfast?' asked Aslam with a huge grin.

'Yes,' said nawabsaab, smiling. 'Breakfast in Dilli.'

Who's Afraid of Ghosts?

The old haveli stood in a forgotten little gali that curved behind the Sunehri Masjid on the busy thoroughfare of Delhi's Chandni Chowk. It had been empty for so long that people had forgotten its name, and they all called it bhoot ki haveli—the ghost's mansion. It stood dark and silent behind high walls. There was an unkempt garden in front, full of bushes and tall grass. Birds nested in the mango trees and squirrels played in its leafy branches. Beyond lay the porch where the grass and creepers had taken over. The windows were shuttered, the doors closed and huge honeycombs hung from the corner of the veranda with the bees buzzing like guards to discourage intruders.

Munia and her two older brothers Khuttan and Dholu loved playing in that wild garden. Here no one yelled at you if you climbed a tree and gathered the raw, tangy mangoes, and as long as you kept an eye out for snakes, you could have a great time playing hide and seek among the bushes. But they never ever ventured towards the house, not even to peer through the wooden shutters of the windows. Everyone said that a very unfriendly ghost lived there. As Dholu said, 'Maqbool, the police hawaldar, no problem. Badlu Ustad, the wrestler, that's alright too, but ghosts with swords? You can't fool them!'

One morning during the summer holidays, Khuttan was busy dusting the shelves of his father's grocery store, which was right across the lane from the haveli, when he saw the men arrive. He yelled to Munia and Dholu as this was something he didn't want them to miss. Obviously the men were masons, carpenters and labourers because they came carrying bamboo ladders, bundles of brushes, trowels, hammers, saws and large flat bowls for mixing the cement. The children looked at each other. What was happening?

In a flash they had streaked across the lane and scrambled over the wall. The men had stacked their things in one corner and were looking around. Then one man began hammering at the ancient lock hanging from the front door. The lock didn't break but with a loud crack the rotten wood of the doorframe itself came apart and the door swung free. Using a broom to clear the cobwebs festooned across the passage, the man went in. He became the first human to have entered the haveli in years.

The children wandered over to a man sitting on his haunches lighting a beedi. Dholu asked, 'What's happening, chacha? Is the haveli being demolished? Have the builders bought it for a shopping complex?'

'Nah,' the man stuck the beedi between his teeth and began to scrape the floor with a trowel. 'We're repairing it. The new owners plan to move in next month.'

'You mean,' Munia's eyes widened in surprise, 'someone wants to live here?'

'Why not?' the man looked up, squinting behind the beedi smoke. 'Good house in Chandni Chowk, just needs to be fixed.'

'But a ghost lives here!' the three of them said together. 'Don't you know?'

The man laughed, showing large yellow teeth. 'Ghost, eh? Whose ghost? Mirza Ghalib's?'

'A nawab's, of course. They say he wanders about carrying a bloody sword ...'

'People who go inside never come out ...'

The man's grin widened. 'Then I better get a sword too.'

'You don't believe us.'

'You don't believe in ghosts?'

The man shook his head, 'No, I don't, and children like you shouldn't either. Anyway, how old is our ghost?'

'Oh! Hundreds and hundreds of years,' Khuttan said vaguely because in fact he didn't have a clue.

'Well, if he is that old, he must have gone to heaven by now.' The man got up and walked through the haveli door. Then he turned to look at them. 'Want to come in?'

Three small heads shook vigorously. 'No, thank you.'

'As you wish,' and the man vanished into the gloom of the ghostly haveli.

By lunchtime the news had spread like wildfire down the gali that someone had actually paid good money to buy that bhoot ki haveli and was foolhardy enough to want to live there! Bashir, the cobbler who was always the first to get all the interesting news, said he had heard that the new owners were from Hyderabad and were planning to start a business in Delhi.

'That explains it,' said Dulari firmly, as she stood leaning against her broom. As the gali's only sweeper, she always had something to say. According to Munia, she was also the slowest sweeper in Chandni Chowk, as she had no time to finish her work after all the chatting and gossiping. 'Hyderabad is so far away, they know nothing about the bhoot.'

'But what does this bhoot do?' Khuttan wanted to know. 'Does it kill people?'

'What does it look like?' asked Dholu, thinking of all the ghosts and vampires he watched in the TV horror shows. Most of them were not scary at all.

There was a thoughtful silence and it was quite clear to the children that no one had the foggiest idea what the ghost actually looked like or did, except that it carried a bloody sword.

'Who knows?' Dulari gave a dramatic shiver and said a quick prayer under her breath. 'You can't trust those things. Their feet point backwards and their heads go round and round like a top and their breath smells of smoke.'

'Doesn't sound too scary to me,' said Munia, swinging her pigtails. 'If I smoked a cigarette, my breath would smell of smoke too.'

Next morning the children were in the haveli garden even before the men had arrived. The men had done quite a lot of work the day before. The doors and windows were open, the cobwebs, honeycombs and bird's nests had been cleared. They had begun chipping and scraping off the old plaster from the walls. Broken bricks and pieces of wood lay in a heap in the garden.

The man who chatted with them the day before was the head mason named Farid. Spotting them under the mango tree, he said, 'You three again? Wanted to check if the ghost had got us or what?'

'Umm ... er ... not really,' Dholu mumbled, going a bit red in the face because that was exactly what he had been thinking.

'Sorry to disappoint you,' Farid lit his first beedi of the day. 'No bhoot, no hidden treasure, nothing. We checked all the rooms.' His lips curved in a smile. 'Want to take a chance and go in? It's an interesting haveli. There's still some old furniture and paintings for you to see.'

Khuttan looked doubtful. 'Maybe later.'

By then Munia's curiosity had grown beyond her fear. 'Let's go, bhaiya, please.' Then, noticing her brothers' nervous faces, she pointed to Farid and said, 'He's alive, isn't he?'

Farid laughed. 'The door's open ... walk straight in.'

Hearts thudding, throats going dry, they took deep breaths and marched resolutely into the bhoot ki haveli. Farid watched them go with amusement. They entered a courtyard with rooms all around it. The sitting room, the baithak, was the large room on the right. It had a high ceiling. A few dusty paintings still hung on the wall. Some pieces of furniture were piled in a corner. Munia ran her fingers over the smooth dark wood and said in wonder, 'Look at this chair—the carving is like wooden lace!'

Eyes wide with delight, they wandered from one dusty room to another. Many were empty but in some there was furniture and rolls of rotting carpets. Chandeliers festooned with cobwebs hung from the ceiling. Khuttan found a brass candlestick with delicate enamel designs and wondered if Farid would let him keep it. Outside they could hear the men at work clearing the garden. Some men began to scrape the baithak walls.

By then they had reached one of the back rooms where the men had not done anything except open the windows. It must have been a bedroom once. A high bed stood in the middle of the room. Tracking footprints across the dusty floor, they looked around. Munia stood in the middle of the room, hands on her hips, and said sternly, 'Ha! Farid chacha was right—there is no ghost here. None at all.'

'Actually you are wrong,' a nervous quavery voice spoke behind them. 'If there are no ghosts then what am 1 doing here?'

Hearts thumping, they whirled around and then saw him. Standing in the darkest corner of the room was an old man, a smudge of light like a pale shadow in the gloom. He was a picture in snowy white hair and beard, wearing a pale kurta and pyjama. He seemed to waver and sway like a picture under water. As they squinted at him to see, the image became firmer as he took a few tottering steps towards them, leaning on a walking stick. A pair of anxious eyes peered out of a deeply lined face. He spoke again in that shaky, worried voice. 'I have to be a ghost, you know.'

The children were so surprised at his appearance that they even forgot to feel scared. Noticing their puzzled faces, the old man waved a thin hand laden with rings before his face and bowed low. 'Nawab Salim-ud-din Masood at your service. Adaab!'

Not to be outdone, Dholu bowed just as elegantly, though his shirt was rather grimy and he hadn't had a bath. 'Salaam! I am Dholu and this is my brother Khuttan and this, my sister Munia. So pleased to meet you.'

Munia came straight to the point, asking impatiently, 'Are you really a ghost?'

'I'm not too sure.' The worried frown was back on the nawab's face. 'What year is it? And who is our king?'

The children looked a bit stumped and then Khuttan said hesitantly, 'It's 1996 … and actually we don't have a king. You see, we have elections …' he began to explain, '… we have a Prime Minister …'

'A mere Prime Minister!' Nawabsaab's eyes widened in horror. 'Have the great Mughals come to this!'

'Er … no … not the Mughals,' Dholu corrected him. 'They are usually Congresswallas and the BJP. Even our local MP …'

Then it hit them. 'Mughals?! Eek!' Three pairs of scared eyes stared at the nawab.

'Mughals!' Dholu thought in panic. 'Then he must be a ghost!' Backing away nervously, he said very carefully, 'The last Mughal died years ago, huzoor. Which Mughal are you talking about?'

'Badshah Bahadur Shah of course!'

'Oh no!' Munia said in horror. 'Then you are really a ghost. The Mughals ruled thousands of years ago!' Her history had always been a bit shaky. 'Bhaiya, run!'

As the three of them turned to flee, the pleading voice of the old man stopped them. 'Please, please don't go. I won't scare you, I promise. Look, I don't even know how to scare the pigeons away when they sit on my head, and you are children … please …'

Three doubtful faces studied him carefully and then Khuttan asked sternly, 'No scary moaning?'

'No no.'

'No bloody sword?'

'Of course not! I hate swords. And where will I get a bloody one when I never fought in a war? Actually the only ghostly thing I can do is vanish …' A smile flickered around the nawab's lips. 'Therefore I must be a ghost. Look!' and he turned and walked through the wall and came back again. 'And see this!' Suddenly he was standing at the other end of the room. 'This is not scary, is it? I do this all the time and I don't know why I do it. I don't even like doing it anymore. It's so boring.'

'Should be,' Dholu said sympathetically. 'The same stupid vanishing trick for hundreds of years.'

The children were having so much fun, they had forgotten to be afraid. It was hard to be scared of this gentle old man who only wanted to chat with them. Munia had checked all the ghostly qualities that Dulari had mentioned, and didn't find any. His feet pointed in the right direction, his head wasn't twirling and he smelled musty, like an old quilt, not of smoke. She sort of liked him.

Nawab Salim-ud-din tottered across the room to sit on the bed with a tired sigh. 'These old bones get tired so quickly. Walking through walls really makes them hurt.'

'Arthritis, I suppose.' Munia said knowledgeably. Her grandmother had it. 'Is it the knees?'

'Yes. And this dust makes me sneeze too.'

'Well, if it's all so painful, why don't you stop being a ghost?'

'I can't! Ghosts can't vanish just like that!' the nawab protested. 'We have our duties too, you know. We are supposed to guard treasures, but my memory is so bad, I can't remember where it is hidden. Or if there is any treasure at all. And I'm so tired of searching.'

'Then stop looking,' Khuttan suggested. 'If you haven't found it yet, you'll never find it.'

'That's the problem. All the other ghosts tell

me that as a house ghost, it is my duty to guard treasures.'

'What other ghosts?' Dholu asked eagerly. By then they were all settled comfortably at one end of the bed, with the nawab sitting like a pale cloud at the other. 'There are more ghosts in this haveli?'

'There are ghosts at many places in this lane. There's the tree ghost in the mango tree in the haveli garden and the well-ghost lives in the dried up well behind the temple. He also visits the hand pump nearby because he is supposed to be a ghost of the water supply department. And now we have a young, new lady ghost ...'

'What do you call her?' Munia wanted to know. 'A ghostess?'

'Where does she stay?'

'She says she likes hanging out in the "Pretty TV & Video Parlour". She likes films, she tells us.'

'Ah! A TV ghostess?' Munia looked delighted. The boys laughed.

'You think it's funny, huh? But they are the only friends I have. We meet often for a chat. Last time we ...'

They heard footsteps outside. Men's voices, the clatter of a ladder being dragged through the corridor. With a start, the nawab sprang up, rushed to the door to peep out, rushed back and whispered, 'Have to go! I hate meeting adults. I'll see you tomorrow. Meet me in the rooftop barsaati room in the afternoon. With a long step he went up to the dark corner where they had seen him first, and then stepping through the wall, he vanished.

Feeling a bit dazed, the three of them wandered out of the haveli. Coming out into the sunny garden, they stared at each other. Had they been dreaming? Munia shook her head. 'How can the three of us dream the same thing at the same time?'

'Maybe that old man was trying to fool us with his tall tales,' Khuttan said, a little doubtful.

'He walked through a wall thrice.'

'And he was across that big room in one huge step.'

'Maybe he is a magician?'

'Maybe!'

Dholu looked around. Everything looked so normal. Who would have thought they had probably just met a real, true-blue, nawabi ghost? Farid and his men were busy working around the house, the pigeons sat cooing on the parapet and the fat brown tomcat sat sunning itself on the garden wall. Dholu turned to the other two and said firmly, 'Don't tell anyone about the ghost. Let's see if he comes again tomorrow. We can check if he is a magician.'

'He can't be a ghost,' said Munia. 'I wasn't scared!'

'Oh yeah? And who said ...' Khuttan mimicked her, 'Bhaiya, run!'

For the rest of the day they kept their secret to

themselves. Luckily, adults don't notice if you are keeping quiet, so no one asked them what the matter was. Dholu helped his father in the shop, weighing out and packing the wheat, rice and spices. Khuttan made some deliveries while Munia helped her mother. Chillies and methi leaves were being dried in the sun and Munia sat guarding them against the birds. All the while their heads buzzed with the morning's extraordinary experiences.

It was evening before they got any time for themselves. Dholu, who was studying Mughal history in school, pulled out his tattered textbook and flipped through the pages. 'Bahadur Shah, he said, didn't he? Bahadur Shah ... here he is ... son of Aurangzeb, became king in 1707 AD.'

Munia pulled an exercise book closer, whipped out a pencil and did some quick calculations. '1996 minus 1707 equals 289. He is really old, bhaiya.'

'Just a minute,' said Khuttan who had been flipping the pages of the textbook. 'There's another Bahadur Shah the second, also with the surname Zafar, who became king in 1837, and got sent off to Burma in 1858.'

'Then he is not that old,' said Munia, busy with her pencil. 'Only a hundred and thirty something.'

It was afternoon the next day when they climbed to the rooftop barsaati room to meet their ghostly friend. Khuttan was convinced no one would be there, and he was proved right. The tiny room was empty.

'Hah! He is not coming,' he said after they had waited a while. 'That old man was fooling us.'

'Ah umm ...' an apologetic voice spoke behind them, 'I er ... forgot ...' and Nawab Salim-ud-din Masood tottered into the room through a wall. 'I was in the garden and I fell asleep.'

'Ghosts don't sleep,' Munia said severely.

'Well, I do. Must be because I'm so old. I usually sleep in the mornings.'

'We don't think you are a ghost, because Bahadur Shah ruled 289 years ago and no ghost can last that long.'

'Or did you mean that Zafar chap? Then you are quite young, a hundred years and something,' Khuttan added.

'Zafar who? My king was the son of Badshah Aurangzeb.'

'Ah!' the three nodded to each other solemnly. '289 then.'

'Allah! I am that old?' the old man's eyes were wide with panic. 'That's why I forget everything!'

'Really?' Munia challenged him. 'We think you're a magician trying to fool us, not a ghost.'

'Oh no, no ... believe me ...' the old man protested.

'Fine, then teach us to walk through walls,' Khuttan said.

'I can't!' the nawab staggered away from them in horror. 'You're alive! You'll hurt yourself. It needs special ghostly skills. I'm not too good either. Once my arm stayed on the other side and I had to go back to get it.'

Three mutinous faces looked at him in disbelief. Then the children told him exactly what they thought of Nawab Salim-ud-din Masood. They said he couldn't possibly be a ghost because his feet pointed in the right direction, his head stayed in place, he didn't smell of smoke and what was worse, they were not scared of him at all. The TV Horror Show ghosts looked scarier than him. Walking through walls was magic, not ghostwork.

The nawab listened to their words quietly and then suddenly clapped a hand on his forehead and said, 'Fool! There is something else I can do. I can go back and forth in time. And I can take you with me.'

'You know such a fantastic trick and you forgot?' Dholu asked disbelievingly.

'But now I remember,' Nawab Salim-ud-din's face was radiant with a smile. 'I can take you back to the time of the three Mughals who ruled from Delhi—Shahjahan, Aurangzeb and Bahadur Shah.' He held out his walking stick. 'Hold on to this, and when I say the magic words, close your eyes. Don't open them till I tell you to do so. If you open your eyes, it won't work. Now which badshah do you want to see?'

'Shahjahan!' they said together.

They held on tightly to the walking stick, eyes clamped shut, and they heard the nawab say the magic words.

Nargisi koftay … dum ki biryani.
Nahari, pasanda, roti bakarkhani.
Chalo aagey!

Suddenly there was a fierce whooshing sound in their ears and it felt like they were flying through a windy, echoing tunnel. One moment they felt cold, next the air was warm. They smelled flowers and incense, frying parathas, cowdung and smoke. Then the nawab's quavery voice told them to open their eyes.

They looked around.

Where *were* they?

It looked like Chandni Chowk, but it was so different. It was clean and the road was not crowded with cars, tongas, rickshaws and buses. There was a channel of clear water running through the middle, with fountains and big shady trees. Palkis borne by men swayed past, men in gorgeous silks rode by on horses and an elephant stood before a haveli. They were dazzled by the beautiful shops and the well-dressed people.

'Where's the "Chamatkar Hair Cutting Saloon"?'

'That pile of garbage in the gali corner is gone!'

'This is the Dilli of my time,' the nawab said with quiet pride. 'See how beautiful the city is? Shahjahan had just built it, and his daughter Princess Jahanara named this road Chandni Chowk—the silver moonlight street.'

'Okay,' said Munia who never forgot what she wanted. 'But where is Shahjahan?'

'Wait—he will come out in procession from the fort to go to the Jama Masjid to say his prayers. Be patient.'

Then they heard the drums, the sound of marching feet and the clatter of horses' hooves, and the fabulous Mughal procession unfolded before them. The nawab explained who the soldiers were—the mace-bearing chobdars, the spearmen called bhalebardars with their spears glinting in the sun, the soldiers playing kettle drums, the gunners and cavalry men. The elephants swayed past with the royal insignia on their back—silver images of the sun and a tiger's head.

Then Emperor Shahjahan came riding in a jewelled howdah on the largest elephant. His son, Prince Dara Shikoh, sat behind him, fanning him with a gold handled fan. They stared at the sharp aquiline face, the large eyes and thin lips. Shahjahan wore a white silk angrakha embroidered in gold, with a triple layered pearl necklace set with rubies. Earrings, turban jewel and rings gleamed in the sun. 'Ah!' thought Muma. 'What a magnificent sight!'

'Much better than the 26th January parade, eh?' Khuttan grinned.

The procession had just gone by when the nawab looked up at the sky and said, 'Oh, I nearly forgot! We have to go back! You can't stay more than one hour. You're alive, after all. Quick, quick! Hold on to my walking stick.' So they clutched the stick and obediently closed their eyes. Then they heard a small voice say, 'Ooops!'

They opened their eyes. 'What's the matter?'

'I can't remember the returning magic words!' the old man wailed. 'What will we do?'

'Think!' Khuttan said desperately. 'I want to go home. I have a cricket match tomorrow.'

'The going forward poem was about nargisi koftay …' Munia prompted him.

'This one is different. Not about dinner at all.' The nawab was beginning to panic. 'You could get stuck here. Oh no … what have I done!'

'Is it a poem on food?' Dholu asked quickly.

'Of course! I only get inspired by food to compose poetry.'

'Lunch … dinner … breakfast … snacks …' they tried to jolt his memory.

'Snacks, of course, I remember! Hold on!' and the nawab recited quickly.

Kebab, chilla, bermi, kachori
Chaat, kulchay aur garam puri
Chalo pichhay!

Again they whooshed through the time tunnel and found they were back in the haveli. 'Now do you believe I am a ghost?' the nawab asked with a satisfied grin.

'Yes!' they said. 'The trip was out of this world.'

'It was, actually,' the nawab gave them a crooked grin. 'And wasn't my time much better than it is now?'

'Then why do you keep coming back?' Khuttan asked. 'You could stay on in that time.'

'But I have to guard the treasures.'

'There are no treasures. You know that. And now Farid bhai and his men will start cleaning up this place and you'll have no place to go.'

'True. What a superb idea! Why didn't I think of this before?' the old man laughed in delight. He became silent, then looked gently at their faces and smiled, 'Goodbye, children, it was great meeting you. Badshah Bahadur Shah, here I come!' and with a whoosh and the soft chant of *Nargisi, koftay, dum ki biryani,* Nawab Salim-ud-din Masood vanished forever.

Dholu, Khuttan and Munia wandered out of the haveli with dreamy smiles on their faces. Farid, the mason, standing halfway up a ladder, plastering a wall, called out, 'Oye! Met the ghost yet?'

'Of course not!' Munia yelled back at him, a mysterious smile playing around her lips. 'And who's afraid of ghosts anyway?'

To Catch a Thief

Rafiq must have said a hundred prayers that evening at the saree satti. The satti was the market in Benaras where the weavers brought their silk sarees to sell to the big dealers. Rafiq's father and uncle were weavers. They wove the famous Benaras silks, all aglow with gold and silver designs. That morning Rafiq and his brother Farid had also come to the satti. It was one of the most important days in the year for their family.

One of the biggest silk dealers, Seth Laxman Prasad was also at the saree satti to select designs. The seth owned big silk shops in Delhi, Lucknow and Agra. Among his customers were rich nawabs and

English ladies. His ships took Indian silks to far-off lands across the seas. Once a year he came to Benaras to look at the new designs. Then he selected a few to add to the collection in his shops. For a poor weaver to be selected by Seth Laxman Prasad meant that he would have regular work for a long time. So naturally, Rafiq was praying and probably Farid was, too.

Rafiq's father unwrapped the cloth bundle and carefully took out six sarees and spread them on the white sheet of the divan on which the seth sat. He showed him the intricate work on the border and the gold motifs on the pallav. After a careful inspection, the seth separated four sarees and asked, 'Have you created them recently? They are not old designs?'

'No huzoor,' Rafiq's father quickly shook his head. 'I made them a few months ago. My brother has helped me weave them.'

'Fine. You'll supply these four designs, in different colour combinations, only on Coimbatore or Chinese silks. Also, I want some lengths of cream silk with buti motifs for my Lucknow shop; it is the new fashion of the nawabs.' He smiled slightly. 'Nawab Wajid Ali Shah wore a silk butidaar achkan, and now all the noblemen will want to follow his example. I want the first batch of silks in three months. Can you do that?' Rafiq's father nodded. 'And I'll buy these four sarees right now,' declared the seth.

Coming out of the room, they sighed with relief, smiling at each other.

'Four designs!' Rafiq's uncle said, delighted. 'I'd never expected him to select so many.'

As they walked past the small shops where the dealers haggled with the weavers over the price of silks, Rafiq said, 'Now we'll have more money, abbu?'

'What will we do with it?' Farid asked excitedly.

'Buy another loom,' said Rafiq's uncle.

'We have to repair the house,' his father said, 'before it falls over our heads in the next rains. I can't have the silk yarn getting wet.'

'A new pair of shoes,' dreamed Rafiq, 'a green kurta with silver buttons.'

'But we have to weave the first batch of silks and we have only three months to finish them,' his father brought them down to earth with a smile.

Going through Sonarpura, crossing a dark, narrow gali, a man hurrying past collided with Rafiq's father. 'Ah! Ahsan Ali! Salaam!'

The man whipped round. 'Yes?' And then his eyes narrowed maliciously, 'Oh! It's you. Heard you got a big order at the satti.'

'Yes. With Allah's blessing.'

'What did you do?' the man gave a crooked smile. 'Stole somebody's designs or tricked the seth and sold him some old ones?'

'Arrey, Ahsan Ali! Why are you so bitter? Next year it will be your turn.'

'Hah!' exclaimed Ahsan Ali and walked away quickly.

Rafiq's uncle laughed. 'The same Ahsan Ali. He'll never do much work but he'll be jealous of other people who do. I heard that last year he was late meeting the sethji's orders so this year the seth did not look at his designs.'

Next morning, twists of silk threads in many gorgeous colours were piled in the two large weaving rooms. The four looms there had been cleaned and oiled. The silk threads were laid out in long lengths to make the warp, and fitted into the looms to be woven into the silk sarees. The shuttles were cleaned and the silk yarn put into them. Rafiq's father, uncle and two assistant weavers worked on the looms. The two boys who were still learning the craft helped them. One of the assistant weavers was late again. Ghulam Hassan wandered in nearly at noon and stood looking bored as Rafiq's father scolded him. He was a tall, thin man and wore a checked lungi, kurta and white cap. He chewed paan, spat into the corner of the courtyard and said, 'I'm good at my work. Does it matter if I'm a little late?'

The boys really disliked the man. He was lazy and rude but they needed him to complete the seth's order. Ghulam was very good at weaving the zari motifs, the little patterns in gold and silver thread. As Farid sat cleaning some shuttles, Ghulam looked up from his loom and said, 'Heard your father got a big order. Which designs were selected? The flower and vine belbuti, the jamdani with the mango motif or the tanchoi?'

'The belbuti and the jamdani.'

'Funny. I didn't think they were all that good. Couldn't the seth find any better designs?'

Farid looked up angrily. 'If you think the designs are so bad, why don't you create some yourself?'

Ghulam moved the shuttle with a clack, checked the pattern on the pallav he was weaving and said, 'Don't worry, bhaiya, I'll do that too and your father will give up designing when I do.'

They worked late into the night and were up early next morning. Farid was cleaning the weaving room when Rafiq carried in glasses of hot milk. 'Ghulam is late again, abbu?'

'I think we have to get another weaver. Ghulam is too troublesome, he argues all the time and he hardly did any work yesterday.'

Rafiq's uncle was looking around and asked, 'Where's the pattern sheet, Rafiq?'

'It was on the table next to your loom.'

Rafiq's father looked up, his face creasing with worry. 'My pattern is not here either.' There was a hush in the room as they realised that something was wrong. And soon they were running everywhere searching desperately for the rolls of paper with the designs. Checking the shelves, around the looms, under the beds. Two of the designs were missing; the two that had not been locked in the box because the men had been working late.

Farid could not still the thought that rose in his mind. 'It must be Ghulam,' he said. 'He was asking me about the designs and he hasn't come to work today.'

'But Ghulam went home quite early. I was still working when he left.'

'No, he didn't,' Rafiq's uncle said quietly. 'I was the last to leave the looms and was closing up when he came back saying he had forgotten to take his lunch bag. I was busy in the other room and didn't see him leave.'

'Boys!' Rafiq's father ordered. 'Run to Ghulam's house and bring him here.'

The boys ran out, and hitching a ride at the back of a potter's cart, reached the lane where Ghulam lived. They ran up the stairs to a small dingy room that Ghulam rented, but stopped in dismay. There was a huge lock on the door.

The landlord who lived on the ground floor was milking his cow and peered out from behind the animal. He said, 'Ghulam? He left suddenly last night. Paid the rent he owed me, packed all the stuff on a tonga and went in the middle of the night.'

'Did you ask him where he was going?'

The man shrugged indifferently, 'I did. But he didn't want to tell me anything.' And he disappeared behind the cow again.

Feeling hopeless, they trudged back home. Now they were sure Ghulam Hassan had stolen the designs, but where could they find him? The rest of the day passed in a haze of worry as they searched everywhere for the missing Ghulam Hassan, but the man had vanished. Doggedly they went on working on the two designs that were left with them, but they knew how strict the seth was. It was quite possible he'd reject the whole order without all four designs. Rafiq's father sat with all his rough drawings trying to remember the final pattern. As the seth had bought the first sarees, he had no sample of the woven patterns to work with either. Next morning being a Friday, the men of the family went to the mosque to say their namaaz. Rafiq knew their prayers were the same. Walking back through the streets full of rickshaws, ambling cows and hawkers yelling out their wares, Rafiq asked his brother, 'Want to come with me? I want to go to Ghulam's house once more.'

'What for? He's gone.'

'I know. But maybe he told someone where he was going. I want to ask around a bit.' The two boys slipped away to the lane where Ghulam had lived. They wandered up and down the alley asking everybody about Ghulam—the paanwala, the man selling earthen pots, the flower seller by the temple. No one knew where the man had gone. Then a shaky voice said from behind them, 'Looking for that good-for-nothing weaver, are you?'

'Yes, Ghulam Hassan,' Rafiq turned anxiously. An old woman sat on a string cot, stitching a quilt.

'Why are you looking for him?'

'He has …' Farid began when Rafiq pinched him to stop him blurting out the truth.

'Well … bibi …' Rafiq stammered, trying to think up a story. 'We live at Mughalsarai. We are his cousins. We had come to Benaras for a few days, and wanted to meet him.'

'He left the night before last. I heard him call a tonga,' the woman smiled, showing broken, paan-stained teeth. 'He told the tonga driver that he wanted to go to Assi Ghat.'

They walked home as it was time for lunch and the family would be waiting. 'Assi Ghat?' Rafiq brooded. 'That's a big place, with dozens of lanes and hundreds of houses. It would take us weeks to find him.'

At lunch, sitting around the dastarkhwan, eating chapatis and korma, Farid asked casually, 'Abbu, do you know anyone who lives near Assi Ghat?'

His father looked up in surprise. 'Lots of people. Let's see … there's my cousin Asad and that old shehnai player Pyare Lal …'

'And Benimadho,' added their uncle, 'who has the sweet shop, and Ahsan Ali who lives around the corner from the shop ...'

'Who?' Rafiq's head shot up.

'That rude man we met the night we were coming back from the saree satti. Ahsan Ali the weaver ...' but before he could finish speaking, the two boys had run out of the room.

As they raced up to the main road, Rafiq panted. 'Let's take a tonga—it'll be faster.'

'Do you have any money?'

'Ammi gave me some to buy coal,' Rafiq replied, waving to a tonga to a stop. They climbed in and sat tensely as the tonga clip-clopped to Assi Ghat which was at the other end of town.

'Where in Assi Ghat do you want to go?' the tongawala asked.

'Benimadho's sweet shop, and hurry!'

'What for? You think the gulab jamuns will be over?'

'No!' said Farid. 'We're going to catch a thief.'

The tongawala turned to look curiously at them. Then as they came to a stop before the sweet shop, he took the fare and said quietly, 'If you two need any help, just yell for me. I'm having lassi at that food shop across the road. Just call out for Sarju.'

They nodded, and going past the sweet shop, they turned at the corner and found Ahsan Ali's house. The door was open and they entered a courtyard where Ahsan Ali was sitting on a string cot, sorting out bundles of silk yarn. The whole house had a run-down ghostly look; the cot had a missing leg and was propped up with bricks. Ahsan Ali looked up with a frown. 'What do you want?'

Rafiq bowed his head and said, 'Adaab, Ali sahib. We are cousins of Ghulam Hassan the weaver and we are looking for him. The people at his old house said he was now staying with you.'

'Ghulam?' Ahsan Ali's frown deepened. 'He's not staying here. I think he is ...' and then his eyes narrowed. 'Wait a minute. I've seen you two somewhere.'

Farid tried to smile. 'But we live in Mughalsarai and we only arrived today.'

'Of course!' Ahsan Ali clicked his fingers. 'That night in Sonarpura. You're lying!'

'Ghulam has stolen some of our designs,' Rafiq admitted quietly.

'So? Why have you come to me?' Ahsan Ali suddenly stood up and began to shout. 'Do you think I've hidden him here? And how dare you think I am in league with a thief? Get out! I know nothing about Ghulam or any missing jamdani designs.' He gripped their arms, pushed them out of the house and slammed the door.

'Oh no!' exclaimed Rafiq. 'He recognised us. You know Farid. I'm sure he knows where Ghulam is.'

'Bhaijaan, did you hear what he said just now?' Farid asked, excited. 'He said he knew nothing about the jamdani designs. How did he know which designs were missing? We hadn't said anything about the designs. Let's go and tell abbu.'

'No,' Rafiq said. 'Let's wait. We'll hide in one of those doorways by the sweet shop. If Ghulam comes, then we'll be sure and we'll tell abbu.'

They settled behind a narrow doorway across the lane from where they could see Ahsan Ali's door. It was a long wait and Farid sat watching the activities in the sweet shop. A fat man in a dhoti was making rabri in a huge black iron kadhai over a fire, stirring the thickening milk with a long wooden-handled ladle. This must be Benimadho, he thought, and said, 'Ooh, bhaijaan, smell that rabri!' he took a deep happy sniff. 'Couldn't we have some while we wait? I didn't even finish lunch.'

'Chup! Idiot. Look who's coming down the road.'

They watched Ghulam approach, carrying a bag. He looked around nervously, slipped into the lane and then reached up to knock on Ahsan Ali's door. Then, as if he sensed something, he glanced at the corner and spotted the boys. His face paled with fear and in a flash he turned and began to run. As the boys chased after him, he scrambled into a tonga.

'Quick! We need a tonga too,' Rafiq panted urgently.

'Sarju bhaiya!' Farid automatically yelled out.

Sarju who was in the food shop biting into a samosa looked up and waved at them, shouting, 'Get into the tonga! I'm coming!' Picking up the ends of his dhoti, he came clattering down the road, still holding a half-eaten samosa in one hand. He leapt into the tonga, stuffed the samosa into his mouth, caught up the reins and mumbled, 'Where's the thief?'

'That blue tonga, he escaped in that.'

'Right!' And he yelled at his horse, 'Chalo, Badal, jaldi.'

The two tongas raced down the road, scattering people, cows and goats. As Badal galloped along, Sarju waved his stick and yelled at everyone to move away. A man riding a horse wheeled away, yelling angrily. Two men carrying a palanquin dropped it with a thud, and a woman screamed. The boys sat clutching the sides of the tonga. They had never had such a hair-raising ride before.

As they neared the Dasaswamedha ghat, Badal was getting closer to the blue tonga.

They could see Ghulam's frightened face as he kept turning to see if the boys were following. He was clutching the bag to his chest. Then, as Badal surged ahead, Sarju wheeled the tonga sharply to the left and blocked the path of the other tonga. Ghulam, his eyes round with panic, sprang out and began running as the tongawala began yelling after him, 'Oye! My money! Where are you going?'

Ghulam raced towards the ghat, chased by the boys and Sarju, the puffing tongawala. 'If we lose him now,' Rafiq thought desperately, 'he'll disappear forever.'

Sarju began to yell, 'Roko, chor! Stop, thief!' Ghulam, panicking, began to head towards the ghat steps that led down to the Ganga, running past the beggars, flower sellers and the pundits sitting under the round umbrellas. Below the steps, the Ganga was full of people bathing in the water. Ghulam began sprinting down the steps.

'Is he planning to jump into the river?'

'But we can't swim!'

'He'll get a boat,' Sarju panted.

'I have no money for a boat!' Rafiq's eyes were wide with panic.

It wasn't easy running down the long flight of stone steps. They were slippery with mud and full of pilgrims who kept blocking their way. Farid slipped. 'Oof!' he screamed and went slithering down and crashed into Ghulam who had reached the edge of the water. The two fell in a tangle, with Farid clutching Ghulam's legs. They lost their balance, rolled down and splashed straight into the water. Ghulam began to scream. 'Don't, don't! I can't swim!'

A grinning Sarju pulled the dripping Ghulam out of the water as Rafiq picked up the bag that Ghulam had dropped. He opened it. With surging relief, he saw the familiar rolls of the designs inside.

'Here they are!' his eyes gleamed in triumph as Sarju and the tongawala gripped Ghulam's arms and pushed him up the steps, past the crowd of curious pilgrims.

'Shall we tie him up?' Rafiq asked.

'No need,' said Sarju grimly. 'I'll break his leg if he tries to move. One of you go and get your father.'

When Farid came hurrying back with his father and uncle, Sarju and Rafiq were sitting beside a wet and miserable Ghulam who fell at Rafiq's father's feet and mumbled, 'Forgive me, bhaijaan, I made a mistake. That Ahsan Ali tempted me.'

Rafiq's father looked at him and frowned. 'Now what do we do with him?'

'Make him pay,' said Rafiq's uncle firmly. 'He'll work without pay for a month.'

'Good idea,' said Sarju with an approving smile, 'and kick him once every morning.' Then he asked casually, 'By the way, what did he steal? I forgot to ask.'

'These ...' Rafiq's father took out the designs. 'My new silk patterns. You and the boys deserve a reward. What would you like it to be?'

'Well,' Sarju grinned shyly, 'I have a son just like these boys. Would you teach him to weave? Then he could make a good living. There's no money in driving a tonga.'

'Of course. Bring him tomorrow. He can learn with the boys.'

'Can we have the shoes you have been promising for months?' Rafiq asked.

'And I want rabri!' added Farid, his eyes shining. 'Two plates of Benimadho's rabri. It must be ready to eat by now!'

A Sword for Deva Raya

My father and I were waiting at the door of our home when the soldiers arrived.

We stood watching the three men turn the corner and ride into our lane. I thought of how handsome my Uncle Kartikeya looked. As a commander in the army of the royal minister Saluva Timma, he was an important man, and his bearing showed it.

He wore the silk dhoti and the quilted tunic of a soldier, with a broad sword at his side. An imperious moustache curved across his cheeks and diamonds glittered in his ear lobes. The two soldiers riding behind him wore leather tunics and carried spears that glinted in the sun. Uncle Kartikeya rode up to his younger brother, my father Ballava, and said, 'I hope you are ready with the blade, brother.'

'Of course!' father smiled. 'When have I been late with a sword?'

Uncle Kartikeya got off his Arab horse. I saw the silk bag he was carrying in one hand. My excitement grew as I knew what was inside. I was dying to see it.

Leaving the soldiers outside, we entered the house and walked to father's workshop at the back of the courtyard. Inside, uncle picked up the newly made sword blade gingerly, felt the edge with his thumb and then said, 'Ah, Ballava, this is a truly magnificent blade.'

'The king deserves only the best.'

By then I was becoming impatient. 'Please, uncle, what about the hilt?' My father and uncle laughed. Then uncle handed me the bag and said, 'See it for yourself.'

Carefully opening the silk bag, I put my hand inside and drew out the heavy silver jewel-encrusted sword hilt. I'd never seen anything so beautiful before.

The handle was shaped like the curved head of an eagle. The eyes were two glittering rubies, and the wings that formed the handle were encrusted with diamonds and pearls. As father and I studied the hilt, uncle said quietly, 'Rubies from the East, diamonds from Golconda and pearls selected by Minister Timma himself.'

'I've never seen a better sword hilt,' father said.

'Yes, Ballava. But do remember, this is a secret. No one must know of the sword for Deva Raya.'

'Of course!' father and I said together.

Now let me go back and tell you how it all began. I am Venkata, 15-year-old son of Ballava, the best swordmaker in the kingdom of Vijayanagar. My Uncle Kartikeya is a commander in the army of Saluva Timma, who is the seniormost, very highly trusted minister of our king, Krishna Deva Raya.

There can be no other king like our king Deva Raya. He is loved by all for his kindness, justice and charity. At the same time, he is feared by our enemies because of his great prowess as a conqueror. All the neighbouring kings respect him and pay him tribute. And this is the reason why the city of Vijayanagar is so prosperous.

Recently, King Deva Raya fought a tough war with his old enemy, Adil Shah of Bijapur, and captured the fortress of Raichur. It was a great victory, and to celebrate it, this year during Dussehra the Mahanavami ceremony will be quite magnificent.

Saluva Timma is not just the seniormost minister of Deva Raya but also brought him up and helped him rule when our king was young. He had decided to present the king with a sword on the occasion. And he selected my father to make the blade. Now the sword hilt which was made by jewellers has been brought by uncle so that father can fit it to the blade.

And as Timma wants the present to be a surprise for the king, it is all to be kept very secret. Only my father, uncle and I know about it.

That night after sending the soldiers away, uncle sat watching us work at the fire. The thinner end of the blade was heated red hot and hammered so that it fitted snugly into the hilt. When it cooled, I polished the blade until it gleamed. Then, carefully picking up the sword, father put it into the leather scabbard and laid it on a length of silk. I stood silently, studying the sword in admiration.

Uncle Kartikeya yawned. It had been a long night. Wrapping up the sword, he put it inside a bag and said, 'I think I'll go now, Ballava, instead of waiting for the soldiers to come in the morning. Timma is anxious to see the sword tomorrow.'

'Don't go alone,' father said and then pointed towards me. 'Take Venkata with you. That's a very precious sword, brother.'

I went out, unhitched our old horse and was ready to accompany uncle to Minister Timma's palace.

This was a few hours to dawn when even the owls and bats seemed to be asleep. We rode through the silent streets of Vijayanagar. Once in a while a watchman would go past, tapping his stick. Far away to the right I could see the fire on top of Hemkutam Hill. It is lit every night to guide travellers to Vijayanagar and also to let our enemies know that Vijayanagar is always awake.

The beat of the horses' hooves was the only sound on the road as we went past dark houses and under the gateways. Soon we were riding beside the Tungabhadra river, the water glinting in the moonlight. I was feeling happy and a bit lightheaded. I was dreaming of what Saluva Timma would say when he saw the sword and what rewards he would give to father and uncle.

We turned a corner and suddenly some men were upon us. Before I could get my wits together, one of them snatched the reins from my hand and pulled me to the ground. 'Help, Venkata!' I heard uncle yell and then all I remember is that I was struggling to free myself from the shadowy men. I could see uncle grappling with the others. I was unarmed, but uncle had pulled out his sword when one man yelled, 'Look out, Ramappa!' I heard the clang of sword blades. Scratching, biting, kicking, I struggled to free myself from the man's grip, thinking all the while that somehow I must get Deva Raya's sword away from the men.

I bit into the man's arm and, with a curse, he pulled his arm away. I was free, running towards uncle. Seeing me rushing to him, uncle threw the cloth bag with the sword to me, shouting 'Run!' Leaving him to fight the men, I whipped around and began running desperately towards Timma's palace. I was running so fast, my feet barely felt the road. But my heart sank as I heard the horses' hooves behind me and knew they were following me.

I ran and ran until my breath came in strangled gasps, but they kept closing in. Soon they were on me. Two men sprang from a horse, one man dived for my ankles, making me trip and go crashing to the ground. The bag flew out of my hand and fell on the road with a clatter. The other man ran to pick it up as the first held me back.

I twisted and turned in his grip and then my hands scrabbled at his face and neck. My fingers felt a necklace around his throat and as I gripped and pulled, it twisted, broke and came in my fist. Just then the other man yelled, 'I've got it. Let's go, Ramappa!'

The man pushed me and ran towards the horse. I saw him spring up behind the man who was carrying the bag. Before I could struggle up, they had galloped away. I had lost Deva Raya's sword.

My body was aching from the fall. Arms and legs bruised and bleeding from scratches, I painfully pulled myself upright and then stumbled back the way I had run. I had to find Uncle Kartikeya. I prayed for him, hoping he was not grievously hurt.

I found him lying on the road and my heart sank when I saw how still he lay. They had hit him on the head. He was unconscious, but there seemed to be no serious wounds. I ran down to the river and wetting my uttariya in the water, came back and wiped his face. To my relief he opened his eyes and struggled to sit up.

'The sword! Venkata, the sword?'

'They took it from me, uncle.' I felt my voice shake. 'They were on a horse and I couldn't run fast enough.'

He sat there holding his head. 'But how did they know about the sword?'

'I don't know.'

'Ballava, you and I were the only people … Saluva Timma had told no one.'

'What about the jewellers who made the hilt?'

'I don't think so. It was made months ago in far-off Madura. The jewellers were not told where the hilt was being taken.'

'Someone in Timma's palace?'

He was silent for a while. 'Perhaps they overheard us … but I was so careful!' he sounded angry and disappointed. I tried to remember the faces of the robbers, but they were masked. 'It was dark. You wouldn't recognise any of them.' Uncle just shook his head. 'There were three men. One stayed back to fight with me while the other two went after you.'

There was nothing more to do except go home. As I helped Uncle Kartikeya get up, my foot stepped on something, and bending, I felt the pieces of the necklace lying on the ground. Remembering I had pulled it off the throat of one of the robbers, I must have still been clutching the pieces when I reached uncle and dropped them beside him. I picked up the beads and the gold pendant and tied it to my dhoti.

Our horses had bolted long ago, so we trudged home, tired. Hearing our stumbling footsteps and broken calls, father, mother and my sister Durga came running out, holding up the lamps. I heard amma and Durga gasp when they saw us.

Slowly we told them what had happened and I saw their faces freeze in horror. Amma, who was tending to our wounds, looked up, her eyes worried. 'Now what will happen to us?'

'First we have to tell Saluva Timma,' uncle said with a sigh. 'He is a fair man but has a terrible temper. If he thinks I betrayed his trust, then I fear for my life.'

'And I fear for mine,' father added.

'Why?' Durga asked.

‘He could think Ballava and I have stolen the sword. After all, no one else knew about it. I can only beg him to give us a chance to search for it.’

‘Oh Devayya, help us, dear lord,’ I heard amma whisper a prayer.

Durga was looking at me, her eyes glittering in the flickering lamplight. ‘We have to find it.’

I understood. This did not just concern father and uncle. It concerned all of us. Our fate was now tied to the sword of Deva Raya. We had to search too.

‘Yes,’ I agreed softly to myself and looked down at the broken pieces of the necklace in my hand.

None of us slept much that night. My father and Uncle Kartikeya sat up trying to think of various plans to hunt down the robbers, knowing well that it was nearly impossible to find them in a city as big as Vijayanagar.

Dawn was breaking when my cousin Ranga came rushing in search of his father. Uncle Kartikeya was supposed to have been home by night. He stopped at the threshold, his eyes widening in surprise as he saw our dazed faces, the bandage on uncle’s head and my scratches and bruises.

By then father and uncle were ready to leave for Saluva Timma’s house. They had to inform him immediately about what had happened. Minister Timma would be even less pleased if they tried to hide the robbery from him. Durga and I were left to tell Ranga of the happenings of the night before. Ranga heard us through in silence and then began asking questions.

I must explain here that Ranga is very different from me, even though we are the best of friends. I am happiest working with my hands and plan to be a swordmaker like my father. But Ranga has no plans of becoming a soldier like Uncle Kartikeya. What he loves are books and mathematics. Uncle says Ranga will become the king's accountant one day. So now I tried to keep up with Ranga's flowing fountain of impossible questions. 'Did you see their faces?'

'No, they were masked.'

'What kind of clothes were they wearing?'

'The usual I suppose,' I said, irritated. 'It was so dark, Ranga, it was difficult to see!'

But Ranga wouldn't stop. 'They spoke our language?'

'Of course! They spoke Telugu,' I said shortly.

'How do you know? Did they say something to you?'

I sat up. Ranga was right! How was I so sure they spoke Telugu? I thought back to the night and then I remembered.

'One of them yelled "Look out Ramappa!" ' I said.

'A Vijayanagar man called Ramappa,' Durga joined in thoughtfully. She is as bad as Ranga, always writing poetry and dreaming. She asked, 'And did this Ramappa wear the necklace?'

'Necklace? What necklace?' Ranga leaned forward eagerly.

I took out the beads and the pendant of the broken necklace and told Ranga how I had pulled it off a robber's neck. And while talking I remembered more. 'Yes, Ramappa wore the necklace. The other man called him by this name when they escaped on the horse.'

Suddenly my heart filled with hope. Now we knew one robber's name! Until Ranga with his logic poured some cold water over it. 'There must be hundreds of Ramappas in Vijayanagar. It's a common name.'

'Of course. But someone will know a Ramappa who wore this necklace,' Durga said thoughtfully.

'And how do you plan to find that out?' Ranga asked sarcastically.

'We ask jewellers, of course!' I said in sudden inspiration and pointed to the pendant. 'Look! This has quite an unusual design, and it's made of gold, so it must have cost quite a bit. Maybe the jeweller who made it will remember who bought it.'

Durga and Ranga were looking at me, surprised, respectfully. They were supposed to be the clever ones, remember?

'Let's go in search now!' I said. 'There are only four days left for the Mahanavami ceremony.'

Our fathers were still not back when we three left the house on our search for the jeweller. It was going to be a long walk. Our houses are in the area where the artisans of Vijayanagar, the potters, ironmongers, woodcarvers and weavers live. The jewellery shops are on the main thoroughfare of the city.

Taking a shortcut through the rocky tracks past the Matanga Hill and jumping over the boulder-strewn path, we walked under the gateways of the walls that surrounded our city. Between the outer walls there are fields and orchards. The villas of the noblemen stand surrounded by gardens and waterways. And in the heart of the city are the king's many palaces, and the Paan Supari rasta, Vijayanagar's most famous road. Visitors from other lands, like the Portuguese horse traders from Goa, say our city is one of the most beautiful in the world.

If you are looking for the jewellery and silk shops, flower arcades and perfume stores, galleries where dancers and musicians perform, you have to come to the Paan Supari rasta.

The closer we got to inner Vijayanagar, the more crowded the roads became. Teeming with hurrying people and horsemen, bullock carts creaked past laden with grain, vegetables and fruit. At the food shops they were lighting the cooking fires and filling the air with pungent smoke. And suddenly I realised I was famished. 'I'm hungry.' Ranga echoed my thoughts. Shall we eat something first? The shops won't be open yet.'

We counted the few copper coins that we had and then ordered bowls of hot milk and fresh bananas. Then sitting outside the food shop we planned our strategy. As Durga rightly pointed out, no jeweller would take us seriously or be patient enough to answer our questions, in his rich shop. We looked too poor to be customers.

'We have to tell a tale,' I said. 'If we just walk in and show the pendant and ask if the jeweller made it, he'll just shoo us away.'

'We'll say we found it somewhere ...' Ranga began.

'And want to return it to the owner!' Durga concluded. 'Very simple!'

'Sounds simple,' I said. 'Let's see if they believe us.'

By then we had finished eating and began walking again. It was around noon when we reached the Paan Supari rasta. The broad thoroughfare was humming with life. Noblemen and their ladies in silks and jewels were getting out of decorated bullock carts to enter the shops. The flower shops laden with Vijayanagar's famous roses and incense stalls were filling the air with fragrance. At the paan shop the woman at the counter was chatting and laughing with her customers as she folded the betel leaves, filling them with nuts and spices.

We stood dazzled by the sights. A tall nobleman in crisp cotton, white and gold antariya-dhoti, his neck and ears glittering with jewels, went past with a servant holding a leaf umbrella over his head to shield him from the sun. A noble lady leaving a cloth shop wore a silk uttariya. The thin veil wrapped around her was set with pearls and her arms and fingers were laden with jewels. Durga sighed, 'Oh, to be rich one day!'

'I will be,' Ranga said. 'I'm going to be a merchant-adventurer, sailing the seas to the east to sell spices, sandalwood and silks to people of faraway lands.'

'And I'm going to work in the king's palace,' Durga said. Then they looked at me and grinned. 'And Venkata will make swords!'

Then we stopped. We were standing before a jeweller's shop. I took a deep breath and asked the others, 'Shall we go in?' Durga and Ranga nodded a bit nervously.

We walked into a small room with a broad divan on which the jeweller sat leaning on a bolster. A lady had just finished paying for a pair of gold bangles. The jeweller put them in a silk bag and bowed low as she got up to go. Then he turned to the three of us as we stood waiting, and said with a frown, 'Yes?'

'Sir,' I began nervously, 'we need your help.'

'Help?' His brows knitted in irritation. 'Go away. I don't give to beggars.'

'No,' Durga stepped forward with her most charming smile. 'We need your help to return a necklace.'

'Return a necklace?' his dark, well-fed face was suddenly interested in Durga's strange words. 'What do you mean?'

By then I had laid the pieces of the necklace, the beads and the gold pendant before him as we told him our planned story. How a man fell off a horse in front of our house and we'd helped him go on and then we found the necklace after he had left. It looked very expensive and we wanted to return it to him. Would the jeweller kindly tell us if he knew of anyone who had bought such a necklace?

The man picked up the pendant and turned it round in his hand and said, 'It's not made by our craftsmen.' His lips curled into a smile. 'We produce better work than this. It's quite crudely made. See!' He pointed to the design. 'It has not been finished properly either.'

'Would you know the jeweller who sells pendants like this?'

'Try the smaller shops in the back lanes. They sell cheap work like this. The jewellers on this road would not make this.' And then as we thanked him and began to leave, his eyes twinkled as he said, 'I don't know why you're looking for the man who wore this necklace. Still, best of luck!' With a mumbled reply, we rushed out of the shop. On the road, Ranga said breathlessly, 'He didn't believe the story! He guessed we'd made it up.'

Still, we had to go on trying. The sword of Deva Raya and the fate of our fathers were at stake. We walked to the lane behind the main road and discovered a row of small jewellery shops. With practice our story must have sounded better because no one else questioned it. Most of them were irritated by our questions but still did admit that they hadn't sold such a necklace.

Then, at the fourth shop, the jeweller, about to shake his head, took a second look at the pendant and said, 'Just a moment! Yes, this is from my shop.'

'Oh!' Durga breathed. 'Who did you sell it to?'

'How can I remember that? It must have been months ago. I don't know all my customers.'

All the while his assistant had been sitting behind him, counting a pile of coins. Suddenly he looked up and said, 'The man had red hands.'

'What?'

We all turned in surprise to look at him. Pouring the coins into the bag, the man said, 'I remember selling that necklace because the man who bought it had hands stained red.' And since we continued to look puzzled, he said reluctantly, 'That's all I can remember. A tall muscular man, his hands looked like he'd dipped them in colour nearly upto his elbows.'

We three were very puzzled and confused as we walked home. We had found the jeweller but the answer was so perplexing, it did not help our search at all.

'A man called Ramappa with hands stained red,' I said thoughtfully. 'It's not enough to find him.'

'I know,' Venkata sighed. 'I had hoped Ramappa would be an old customer that the jeweller would remember and could tell us where he lived.'

We walked on in silence. I was feeling really tired. After all the excitement of the night and the long trek in the morning, my legs felt heavy as stones. The bruises on my arms ached. When we reached home we found amma and my aunt sitting silently in the courtyard. Their faces told me that the news was not good.

'Where's appa?' Ranga asked.

Seeing our anxious faces, amma tried to sound cheerful. 'It's not so bad. The minister Timma believed your father ...'

'Not really,' my aunt interrupted her. 'He has just not put them in prison for the theft. Your fathers have to stay in the palace under guard while Timma's soldiers search for the sword. He has given them up to Navami to find it.'

I sat down slowly, disappointment seeping into my bones. I had hoped to tell father and uncle about our discoveries and ask their advice. Now it looked like we'd have to search for Ramappa ourselves.

Leaving Durga and Ranga to tell amma and Aunt all the news of the day, I tumbled inside and lay down. All the while the jeweller's words ran through my head. 'Hands stained … hands stained red …' And the last thought in my head as I dropped off to sleep was, 'Who has stained hands?' And still wondering, I dozed off.

Next morning, Ranga, Durga and I stayed home while amma and my aunt went to Saluva Timma's palace to see if they would be allowed to meet father and Uncle Kartikeya.

We sat in the workshop surrounded by the things used by my father for his work. It was so sadly silent, when usually it echoed to his hammerings. The tongs, hammer and chisel lay idle, the fire pit was no longer alive with glowing hot coals. I asked the question that had been running through my head constantly, 'Who has stained hands?'

'A painter?' Durga wondered and then shook her head. 'Not the way the man described it—dipped upto the elbow in colour.'

'Maybe he makes colours,' I said, 'or paints walls.'

'Of course!' Ranga suddenly sprang up in excitement. 'He must be a dyer!' Then noticing our puzzled faces, said, 'Haven't you seen men dipping rolls of thread and newly woven cloth into big buckets of colour?'

'Yes! In the weavers' locality.'

'Let's go!' I yelled, and in a moment we were out of the house and heading towards the corner of

Vijayanagar where the weavers stayed. I was feeling hopeful again. At least we could now try to find a man called Ramappa who dyed cloth, and if such a man existed, we were on the right trail.

You can always hear the weavers at work from far away. There is the rhythmic wooden "click clack" of their looms. In the weavers' locality we entered the narrow lanes between the thatched huts. All around us, multi-coloured threads of silk and cotton were drying on walls and hedges. Newly woven sarees and cloth lay in neat packages on the verandas of the huts where women sat rolling thread into spindles. The wooden spindles whirling in their hands went round and round ceaselessly.

I put my head inside a hut where a man sat weaving at a loom and asked, 'Where can I find Ramappa, the dyer, sir?'

The man looked up and said, 'At the end of the lane.' I felt my heart thud! The weaver was still speaking, 'But I suggest you get another dyer. Ramappa is not a man to be trusted.'

Standing in the lane, we three stood and stared silently at each other. Devayya, the lord be praised, it seems we were on the right trail. A dyer named Ramappa who was a suspicious character. But was he the man who had stolen the sword?

We talked about what to do next. We couldn't catch him ourselves and it would be foolish to go up to him. If he was the robber he would hardly admit that to us. And if he got suspicious, he would vanish before we could get the soldiers. Finally we decided to take a look at him and then go back and tell our fathers everything.

At the end of the cluster of weavers' huts a boy pointed out Ramappa's house. It was a small hut with a courtyard where a large copper vessel was smoking on a coal fire. A man with his back to us was stirring the contents with a stick. We slid behind a thick hedge and sat watching him through the leaves.

The man leaned forward and dipped a roll of cotton into the boiling colour and then pulled it out. It was now dyed blue, and the man turned to put it to dry over the courtyard wall. I caught a glimpse of his face. He was a tall muscular man with a bony, angry-looking face, like the man that jeweller's shop assistant had described. If this man had held me that night, I could never have escaped with the sword. He was twice my size and looked very strong.

I was wondering what to do next when Ramappa went over to a corner and began washing his hands. I noticed his arms were darkly stained upto the elbows. Then wrapping an uttariya over his bare body, he walked out of the house and began going towards the city.

Ranga whispered, 'What do we do now?'

'Follow him. Maybe we'll find out something more.'

Ramappa strode on, walking fast towards the river. We skirted a row of houses and then were on the road that led to the Pampapati temple. We were careful about staying out of sight, walking as far from him as we could. Fortunately the temple road is always crowded with pilgrims, so we could lose him easily.

Abruptly Ramappa turned right and we were in a quiet lane. We stayed back at the corner watching him. He looked around. Quick as a blink we had ducked behind a wall. Peering out, we saw him go and stand by a gateway across the road. For a while he stood waiting. Then, from the other end of the gateway, we saw a man stroll across. He quickly handed him a roll of paper, and without a word, walked on.

'Did you see that?' Durga whispered excitedly.

Ramappa turned and walked towards us, but before he reached the main road, he stopped. He opened the roll, read the letter and tucked the roll at the waist. He hurried back the way he had come, towards the weavers' locality.

'What next?' Durga wondered. 'Looks like he's going home again.'

'What do we do now?'

'We steal the letter.'

'What! Venkata, you're mad.'

'Watch me,' I said and left them standing open-mouthed, too surprised to even try to stop me. By then we were on the main road again. Instead of following Ramappa from afar, I hurried forward until I was walking so close to him that I could smell him. He looked relaxed and walked on carelessly, getting jostled about by the hordes of pilgrims. The crowds to the Pampapati temple grew during Dussehra.

My opportunity came when a battalion of soldiers galloped past, stopping all the pedestrians, making people back away to the side of the road, the noise and dust enveloping us. During all the chaos, with people pressed together, I leaned forward and plucked the letter out of Ramappa's waistband.

Ramappa half turned as if he felt something, but just then a soldier's horse neighed and reared up, making the watching people sway back in panic. By the time Ramappa managed to look around, I had slipped away, waving to Ranga and Durga to follow me quickly.

We ran, zipping through the back lanes so fast that our breaths came in short gasps. We only stopped when we were in the lane leading to our home.

'That … was …' Durga panted, 'quite … fantastic, Venkata.'

'I knew … you were good … with your hands …' Ranga puffed, 'but I didn't know it included … pick-pocketing!'

I just grinned, huffed and puffed.

We reached home to discover amma and aunt waiting anxiously for us. It was late afternoon and we had been out for hours. And were we hungry! Over lunch, they told us of their experiences at Minister Saluva Timma's palace. The search was still on. Father and uncle were out searching in various quarters of Vijayanagar, though without much success. They had found no clue to the identity of the robbers. And worse, Saluva Timma was now beginning to get angry. And then, in between mouthfuls of rice we told them of our adventures during the day.

Amma and aunt listened wide-eyed and then, as we finished our story, they said together, 'What does the letter say?'

'I don't know,' I mumbled, my mouth full. 'I was too hungry to read it.'

'Oh really, Venkata!' Aunt exclaimed impatiently and snatched the roll of paper from my hand. Then she sighed. 'But I don't know how to read!'

By then Durga had finished eating, though I was still munching busily. After washing her hands, she came and opened the roll of paper and began to read -

We await the blade of lightning. Come on Panchami night. We will meet you where the shadow of the tall walls falls across the Tungabhadra and touches the shore.

We looked at each other, puzzled. 'What blade?' I asked.

'What tall walls?' amma wanted to know.

'Lightning over the river?' Aunt's brows were crinkled.

All the while Ranga and Durga had been sitting so still, I could almost hear the click of their clever minds getting to work. Then they bent over the roll of paper, fingers tracing the words, and began to explain what they meant.

'Blade of lightning!' Durga muttered thoughtfully. 'A sword has a blade. This must be their code for the sword. And it does shine like lightning.'

'Tall walls ... tall walls ...' Ranga mumbled. 'Where beside the Tungabhadra River are there tall walls?' And then he grinned at us. 'Of course! The Anegundi Fort! That has the tallest walls in all Vijayanagar and their shadow falls over the river.'

'But the fort is across the river,' I said.

'Exactly!' Durga exclaimed. 'So the shadow falls across the river to this bank where there is ...'

'The Telarigattu Ghat!' Ranga and I yelled together. Suddenly it had all fallen into place. Ramappa was going to sell the sword to some other people and now I knew how to catch the robbers of our Deva Raya's sword.

'So on Panchami night we'll go with father, Uncle

Kartikeya and his soldiers to the ghat and we'll catch them red-handed!' I smiled.

'Oh no!' Amma's eyes were wide with panic. 'But today is Panchami! And it has already become dark. What do we do now?'

For a moment all of us sat still in panic. There had been three men who had attacked uncle and me. And there were the men coming to buy the sword. We couldn't catch them all on our own; we needed help. But was there time to get the soldiers from Saluva Timma's palace?

'Quick!' I said, springing up. It was time for action now. 'Amma, you and aunt run to the palace and get help.'

'But what are you planning to do?' aunt asked anxiously.

'We three will go to the Telarigattu ghat and somehow try to stop the thieves. Now, amma, hurry!'

As amma and aunt hurried away to Saluva Timma's palace, Ranga, Durga and I ran out of the house and raced towards the ghat.

Whatever happened, I was going to get back the sword of our King Deva Raya tonight.

Down the slope, up the hilly path, past the boulder-strewn field, cutting through the backlanes of houses, we ran as if a thousand demons were chasing us.

The roads were dark by now, lit fitfully by the few lamps at the doors of houses, and in our hurry we often stumbled and stubbed our toes. Then turning a corner we were on the road that led straight to the Telarigattu Ghat. Ahead of us I could see the pale sails of the boats tied up at the bank and smell the dank breeze coming from the river. 'Wait!' I yelled urgently, making Durga and Ranga skid to a stop. 'We can't just go rushing in like that. They'll just hit us, tie us up and get away,' Ranga nodded.

'You're right—we have to hide and study the situation first.'

'Let's creep in behind those bushes,' Durga pointed. We stepped away from the road and behind the border of hedges, and bending low, walked silently towards the ghat. The ghat is a huge landing stage where the boats coming up the Krishna River and into the Tungabhadra bring their goods from far off lands like Banga and Kalinga. The boats anchor at the ghat and then the goods are unloaded and carried onto a clear area around the ghat. And just beyond the broad span of ghat steps there were piles of goods lying around. Big bales and large sacks, packets and bundles, baskets and boxes. It was a perfect place for hiding.

We crept behind these piles and went closer and closer to the ghat steps because anyone coming by boat would come that way. Finally we settled down behind a mountain of baskets and peered out towards the river shimmering in the moonlight. Oddly enough I could smell bananas nearby—probably from the baskets around us.

Everything was quiet, the quay was deserted, when Durga suddenly turned her head and whispered, 'I can hear footsteps!' In the silence we could catch the soft crunch of shoes over the stony path. We bent lower behind the baskets. From our hiding place I could hear the steps get closer and closer and go past us. Then a voice said, 'It was stupid of you to lose the letter, Ramappa!' and my skin crawled. This was the voice of the man who had shouted that night!

'It must have fallen somewhere in the crowd on my way back,' a second voice said roughly. 'No one will understand it anyway.'

Tue footsteps went further away. Very cautiously I raised my head to look through a crack among the baskets and saw the two shadowy figures walk up to the bank of the Tungabhadra and stand as if waiting. We sat back and waited too.

All the while we wondered what we could do to stop them from escaping with the sword. It had to be something clever; just the three of us could hardly fight and stop them, especially when Ranga and Durga would rather use their brains and not their muscles! I was still worrying about it when a movement caught the corner of my eye, and turning,

I saw Ranga shove his hand into a basket and pull out a bunch of bananas!

Durga giggled softly as we sat there peeling and eating the bananas. I wondered if the owner of the basket would know some were missing!

I had been keeping an eye on the two men and I noticed that they were suddenly getting active. They were walking up to the edge of the river to look upstream. Then I heard the soft slap of oars in the water and I knew I had guessed right. The buyers of the sword were coming up the river by boat.

We heard Ramappa shout, directing the boat to where they were standing, and then one man leaned forward to pull in the boat by the rope thrown to him. Two shadowy figures got off and the four men stood talking. And then I saw Ramappa hold out a large bundle.

'The sword!' Ranga said. 'Oh, Devayya, where are the soldiers?'

'We have to stop them now,' Durga said urgently, 'before they escape by boat.'

Not knowing what else I could do, I just stood up behind the baskets and began shouting at the top of my voice. 'Soldiers! Here! Catch them!' Ranga and Durga quickly understanding what I was doing began yelling too, 'Quick! The thieves! Don't let them get away!' The three of us jumped about creating a huge din.

The men whirled around to look and then came running towards us. 'What do we do now?' Durga asked in panic, 'Oh! Where are the soldiers?' By then I had started tearing open the baskets. I yelled, 'Throw these! Fast!' In a moment bananas, pears and papayas were whizzing through the air and hitting the men, making them stop dead in their tracks in sheer surprise.

It was a fight to see. As one man came charging at me, I picked up a papaya, jumped on top of a big bale and smashed it on his head with a splat! Another man had caught hold of Ranga who was still yelling for the soldiers. And when he turned around, he stepped on a mess of squashed bananas and went slithering to the ground to land on his back with a loud 'Ooof!'

During all the chaos, clever Durga had run off to the edge of the water and untied the rope to let off the boat that was now drifting away. The men couldn't escape by the river anymore!

But they were four hefty men and we were three children and I knew this was a fight we could never win. The men were getting the best of us when Ranga yelled, 'The soldiers, Venkata! The soldiers have come!' And I can tell you that sound of galloping horses coming towards us was the most beautiful thing I had ever heard in my life.

Hearing the soldiers, the men let go of us and turned to run. The bananas came to our rescue again.

As we tried to stop them, grabbing their ankles, clutching their arms, they would slap and punch us to break free and run, step on a banana and go splat on their back! If we hadn't been so busy fighting, we three would have died laughing.

By then the soldiers holding torches had surrounded us and I saw Uncle Kartikeya and father spring down from their horses to grab the men. Then uncle saw Ramappa's friend and his eyes widened in shock, 'Chaturbhuj, you! How could you do this?'

'Who is he?'

'He's Saluva Timma's chief steward,' uncle said. The four men with their arms and legs tied stood glaring at us.

'Where's the sword?' I ran to the edge of the *ghat* to pick up the bundle lying there. I went up to father and put it in his hand.

Standing in the circle of torches, father pulled open the silk bag and inside we saw the familiar leather and gold scabbard. Then he pulled out the sword and held it up. It glittered in the torchlight. 'The blade of lightning,' Durga said dreamily.

As the soldiers led Chaturbhuj, Ramappa and their gang away, we three very tired and messy children sat down on the baskets with a sigh of relief. It had been a very very long day. Searching out Ramappa, following him, stealing the letter and finally this crazy fruit fight. Father and uncle smiled at us, and pulled us up on their horses. We rode home like real soldiers.

One question that bothered me from the start had now been answered. Timma had believed only Uncle Kartikeya and father knew about the sword, but his steward Chaturbhuj must have overheard their plans. Next day when Uncle Kartikeya came back from the palace, we heard the rest of the story.

Chaturbhuj and his gang planned to send the sword to the kingdom of Bijapur where a jeweller was going to sell it to a prince of Bijapur. The best news of all was that we were invited to attend the Mahanavami celebrations at the palace!

On Mahanavami, Durga, Ranga and I stood admiring each other. We'd never worn such gorgeous clothes before! My silk dhoti was a deep blue while Ranga's was butter yellow. Durga wore a green and gold skirt that made her look like a fluttering butterfly.

King Krishna Deva Raya's palace was so magnificent. As we wandered through it, our eyes dazzled. Tall, carved stone gateways led to large rooms with pillars covered with engraved ivory and silver. The floors were covered with soft carpets and silk curtains swayed in the breeze. The air smelt of sweet incense and flowers. Female guards stood at all the doorways holding spears and swords.

We watched the daylong Mahanavami celebrations. First Deva Raya worshipped the horses in the royal stables, throwing flowers at them as the priests chanted mantras, while elephants covered with rich cloth stood swaying. Then we all went and stood in the Audience Hall where Saluva Timma was going to present the sword.

To the sound of conches and trumpets, the dancing devadasis entered, followed by the two queens accompanied by maids holding lamps. Then Krishna Deva Raya came striding in to occupy the jewel-encrusted gold throne.

Krishna Deva Raya was clad in white silk, embroidered in gold. Jewels glittered at his throat, ears and arms. His tall jewelled silk crown made him look so regal, we all bowed low to him. Father pointed to an old, white-haired man and said, 'That's Saluva Timma,' and then to a man with bright eyes and an amused smile he said, 'and that's Tenali Rama.' I looked again at the man whose jokes and crazy exploits were repeated all over Vijayanagar. All of us knew a few Tenali Rama stories.

As we watched with thudding hearts, Saluva Timma walked up to Deva Raya and bowed. Behind him, Uncle Kartikeya stood holding a silver salver on which lay the sword.

After congratulating Deva Raya on his great victories at Raichur, Timma picked up the sword and laid it in Deva Raya's hand with a smile. Krishna Deva Raya smiling in return pulled the sword out of the scabbard and held it up for all to see. The room echoed to applause. I glanced at father and saw his face bursting with happiness.

Then Saluva Timma turned his white-haired head towards us and said, Ballava, Venkata, Ranga, Durga ... the Deva Raya would like to meet you.'

In a daze we walked up to the foot of the throne and heard Timma say that Uncle Kartikeya had been promoted while father was now the royal swordmaker. Then he turned to us and the King said, 'And you three are the true children of Vijayanagar. Brave as lions and clever as foxes. What would you like as a reward?'

Tongue-tied, we looked at each other. Krishna Deva Raya smiled and said softly, 'Come closer,' and then he put gold necklaces, set with jewels, round our necks. The room was again filled with shouts of praise and applause.

Our hearts bursting with pride, we walked back to where amma and aunt stood, their eyes shining with tears of joy. Our clever Ranga had the last word. Admiring Durga's necklace, he grinned at us and said, 'Not bad for a banana fighter ... hmmm ... Venkata?'